THE PETROV FAMILY

MIKHAIL

PETROV

ELLE MALDONADO

Editing: **Mackenzie Letson of Nice Girl, Naughty Edits**

Cover Design: **Dream Echo Designs**

Formatting: **Dream Echo Designs**

AUTHOR'S NOTE

…because forbidden tastes a little sweeter
and burns a lot hotter.

CONTENTS

CHAPTER ONE
MIKHAIL

FOUR YEARS AGO

Dallas, Texas

Late.

I hate being late. Lateness is equivalent to laziness. And my reputation and name mean everything to me. As the oldest of my brothers, I'll sit at the head of the table one day, take over my father's business dealings, and rub elbows with the vilest of society's underbelly. Sure, I can demand respect and *take* it, but there's something about earning it that sets a man apart.

The chime of my phone breaks through the low hum of music in my car and pulls me from my thoughts.

"How far out?" Rodrigo's voice blares through the speaker, a loud bass thumping in the background.

"About fifteen."

"Everyone is hungry. We're waiting on your ass."

It's Emilio Castellanos's sixtieth birthday celebration. Rodrigo's father and family have been long-time allies of ours. While I would have instead spent my Saturday night at home, a glass of scotch as company, part of my obligations in Dallas is maintaining relations and alliances. This is an easy task where Rodrigo is concerned since he's more of a brother to me than a business partner.

"I'll be there…" My voice trails off as I catch sight of a smoking car up ahead, its hood raised. Any other time, I'd keep driving, but something interesting draws my rapt attention.

"Rod, I'll see you soon."

Without waiting for a response, I end the call and cross the median, veering onto the shoulder and stopping about twenty feet behind the stalled vehicle. The road is desolate, and the sun has just begun to set. It's not the safest scenario for a woman in such a vulnerable state.

Why I give a fuck is another story.

As I round the hood, a pair of legs—sleek and tanned—in light-colored denim shorts, revealing the underside of a sweet, plump ass, is all I can see as the rest of her is bent over the billowing steam.

My cock twitches as I imagine taking her just like that, out here in the open.

"Fuck, fuck!" she shrieks and pounds the car, clearly frustrated.

"Hey." My tone rushes out, colder than I intended, causing her to stiffen and go quiet. A beat later, she twists around with a Glock trained on my chest. For a fraction of a second, I reach for my weapon until awareness dawns on us both.

"Mikhail?"

Leah Castellanos.

She gasps and holsters her gun, a broad, almost relieved smile lighting up her beautiful face.

Fuck me. She's gorgeous.

Always pretty. But now… she's something else.

A woman.

"Leah."

That's all it takes for her to break and rush me. Tears fill her eyes as she throws her arms around my waist.

I hesitate before returning the hug, uncomfortable with the thoughts I'd had as I pulled up. The ones I'm still having while she's nestled in my arms.

And damn it all, if she doesn't feel perfect.

"I'm so happy to see you. This piece of shit was all they had for rent. It started smoking, and I tried to remember what Rodri taught me, but—"

I cut off her rambling. "It's okay. I'll get you home."

She rests her chin on my chest, and her big brown eyes find mine. "I left my cell at the rental place. Just one disaster after another. I was about two minutes from hitchhiking home."

The thought of Leah getting into some stranger's car fills me with unease.

"That wouldn't have been very smart."

She shrugs. "Well, it was either that or walk the ten miles. But thank God you passed by. Crazy, huh?"

"I was on my way to your father's party— But Leah, I thought you were still in New York. Rod didn't mention you coming."

The last time I saw her was at her high school graduation over a year ago. She's been home for holidays and random visits since leaving for college, but somehow, we never coincided. Eight years younger and the baby of the Castellanos family, I never made it a point to keep in contact. And I certainly never thought of her in any other way.

Until now.

Something fractures inside me the longer I hold her.

"I wanted to surprise everyone. It's why I rented this shitty car instead of having Rodri or Ann pick me up." She smiles and squeezes me tighter, and my cock responds accordingly. If she notices, she doesn't give anything away.

"Come on. It's getting dark. Let's get you home."

Pushing away from me, she shakes her head. "I can't go home right now. I'm too shaken up, and the last thing I want or need is my mom or Ann down my throat."

"Leah, your brother is expecting me. I can't not show up."

I'm a son of a bitch because, despite everything, my eyes are focused on her ass as she walks back toward the wreck and bends under the hood again. The hem of those goddamn shorts slides up just enough to indulge my eyes with the swell of her cheeks. Leah tosses a look over her shoulder and bites her lip. If I didn't know better, I'd say she's doing it purposely to fuck with me.

"I don't want to keep you. A friend of mine is just about an hour away. Let me use your phone, and I'll wait for her. You go ahead—"

"The hell I will."

Leah's head snaps up, her eyes narrowing as she watches me. "Mikhail, I'll be fine," she says, returning to my side and patting the gun at her waist.

My gaze falls to the sliver of smooth skin peeking out from the top of her shorts. I'm so entranced I don't realize she's only inches from me now.

"Your phone. Mikhail?"

"You're out of your fucking mind if you think I'm going to leave you here."

"What?" Vulnerability and confusion flicker over her expression, but she quickly squares her shoulders. "What's your problem?" she asks, poking my chest.

"You're Rod's little sister. I'm not going to just leave you out here while I go back to your place like nothing."

Leah crosses her arms and purses her lips. "Mikhail, I don't know if you've noticed, but I'm not a kid anymore. I can handle myself just fine."

I noticed.

"Are you hungry?" I ask, against my better judgment.

When she smiles, it perturbs me to think that I'm willing to do anything to keep it on her face.

I pull into a parking spot two spaces from the nearest streetlamp, which gives us just the right amount of light versus privacy. Leah unwraps her burger and takes a bite, nodding and voicing her approval through a low moan. To my horror, everything she does elicits a response from below the belt.

"Your sister hires a renowned chef to prepare a buffet of delicious food, yet you insist on eating a greasy burger in a parking lot."

She laughs. "Ann is always looking for an excuse to eat good food and throw a party. It's certainly not the last one, so let me enjoy my fucking burger, okay?"

A smile crawls across my mouth, and I lean against the seat, trying to shake whatever the hell this feeling is taking up space inside my chest. There's no denying my attraction to my best friend's little sister.

"You're not eating?" she asks.

"Nah. I'm not hungry."

Leah touches a hand on my wrist. "I'm sorry I dragged you out here, Mikhail. We can head back as soon as I'm done."

"I'm not in a hurry," I reply, silencing the vibration in my pocket.

Rodrigo's missed calls are stacking up. He's probably wondering where the fuck I am. I don't want to lie to him, nor do I want to tell him I'm with Leah. I'm enjoying this…whatever *this* is.

Enjoying her company in a way I never have before.

"How are your brothers and Nikolai? Haven't heard about them in a while."

"Everyone's good. Doing their own thing. You know how that goes. And Dad is doing better." She nods, understanding alight in her eyes.

The Castellanos have never tried to conceal who they are, not even from Leah. Being so close to Rodrigo, she was always in the mix as far as I can remember. We taught her how to shoot, throw punches, properly use a Kukri knife, and parallel park.

The important things.

But there's nothing left of that girl. She's someone else.

"And you, Mikhail? How have *you* been?"

"Good."

She chuckles. "Such a vague answer. Always a man of few words."

It's my turn to laugh.

"I am good, though. Business is business. Bought a new place. A couple of cars. Low-profile shit."

Leah leans over the center console. "And do you have someone waiting for you…at that new place of yours?"

Mindlessly, I lift my thumb to her lip and swipe at a breadcrumb. We lock eyes, and she slowly glides her fleshy mouth back and forth against my skin.

Fuck.

"No, I don't," I say, my voice low as I drop my hand.

"Not that I'm complaining, but you're quite the catch, Mr. Petrov. Why so lonely? Are you a serial killer or something?"

I can't remember when I've laughed this much with anyone who isn't Rod or my brothers. And I'm not sure how to feel about it. And as far as the single thing goes, she isn't too far off. I don't kill for fun or thrills. Only when I need to. And finding someone who won't call the feds on me isn't practical in the local dating scene.

Celeste Orlova comes to mind.

My father proposed we get married, unite our families, to increase territory and wealth, a commonplace practice in our world. I said yes, simply to appease him and play the part he expects of his firstborn son. Although I've never met her, she's pretty enough, I suppose.

Pretty enough. I roll those words around in my thoughts as I gaze at the striking beauty of Leah Castellanos.

"I just haven't found someone who will put up with me. I'm an asshole."

"Well, self-awareness is the first step," she jokes, playfully patting my thigh.

Again, I find myself smiling like a fucking fool.

"And you? I imagine you have someone missing you back in New York. Look at you… You're beautiful, Leah."

She suddenly reaches for my arm again, fingers tracing the ink there. My eyes fall on her black nail polish, but I feel the heat of her gaze on me.

"I don't. There isn't anyone there that catches my eye. They're…a little younger than what I like."

"Is that right?"

A sense of relief followed by dread ripples through me. I'm not supposed to enjoy that she isn't in a relationship.

Sighing, she lays her head against the seat. "But it doesn't matter anyway, because I'm not going back."

"As in, you dis-enrolled?"

"Exactly. School's just not for me." She twists and watches me with those alluring dark eyes. "I have other interests."

Either I'm just an arrogant son of a bitch, or she's purposely trying to provoke me.

"Your father was so happy when you got accepted. I'm sure that conversation didn't go over too well."

"That's probably true... but I won't know until I tell him."

I rake my fingers through my hair and shake my head. Leah is Emilio's pride and joy, as they say. He has her life mapped out and probably a husband lined up as well. That last thought makes me want to put my fist through a wall—or someone's face, preferably the future husband.

She deserves better.

You're no better.

"Let me know if you need a place to hide until things smooth over."

The moment I speak the words, I realize how they can be interpreted. But I don't correct myself. Instead, I selfishly wait for a response.

"You and me at your place together, Mikhail." She leans into my space and whispers, "Just know I won't be good."

Fuck. Me.

I grip the steering wheel to occupy my hands and keep from pulling her into my lap like any other woman in her place. But this is fucking Leah.

The girl I watched grow up.

"I'm not sure I know what you mean."

"Don't play dumb with me. I'm not sixteen anymore," she says, inching forward, her hand on my thigh.

"Leah... things aren't like that between us. You know they can't be."

Catching her wrist, I stop her strokes and meet the fire in her gaze.

Never one to hold back with someone I want as much as I do Leah, I curse and instead use my aggravation to discourage her advances. "You're Rodrigo's little sister. I can't see you as anything other than that."

"Liar," she whispers. "Your cock is hard for me, Mikhail. And I'm not that stupid little girl with a crush anymore." Her lips brush the shell of my ear, sending a tingle down my spine. "Because back then, I would have never told you how wet my pussy is for you right now."

I suck in a sharp breath. "Oh, fuck."

Without thinking, running purely on sexually driven instinct, I grasp her hips and toss her onto my lap, her warm little cunt settling over my abdomen. Our gazes collide for just a second, lips a breath away, before we crash into each other. When the taste of her spills onto my tongue, it sets every cell within me on fire.

My fingers tangle in her hair, and she moans into my mouth as I tighten my hold and goddamn nearly devour her whole.

"You have no idea how long I've wanted to do this," she pants against my mouth while grinding her hips over my cock.

"Your father will skin me alive," I say, shoving the hem of her shirt above her bra and biting at the pink lace, coaxing her nipple to a peak.

"I won't tell if you don't."

Her words are like a shock of ice water.

"Leah, stop." I pry her hands from around my neck and push open my car door, needing some fucking fresh air. Leah slides off my lap, face twisted into a look of disappointment and something else I can't pinpoint. "What are we doing? This can't happen between us. You and me… No."

"Why not?"

"You know why." I pound the roof of the car and grit my teeth. "Get back in your seat. I'm taking you home."

She scoots into the passenger seat without another word, and I peel out of the parking lot with tires screeching against the pavement.

MIKHAIL PETROV 11

CHAPTER TWO
LEAH

The loud bass reaches beyond the gates of my parents' home, matching the pounding inside my chest as I recover from the adrenaline dump of what happened between us in the lot. My gaze slides over to Mikhail, then down to the gear shift where his knuckles are white and his skin is taut.

I turn away, eyes on the glass as we pull into my drive, suddenly feeling cheap and used, and every bit that stupid girl pining for a man who will only ever see me as his best friend's little sister.

But I've loved Mikhail since I was eleven. And maybe it's a foolish thought since I was just a kid, but every day and every damn year, my feelings for him have grown. This isn't just a crush or some fantasy I need to fulfill. Mikhail Petrov was born to be mine. I know the risks and possible repercussions, but I don't care. Not anymore.

"Thank you."

"You don't need to thank me."

"You saved me today. Of course, I do."

The car comes to a stop, and he finally stretches and flexes his fingers. "Leah, what happened back there... I shouldn't have lost control like that."

"Stop. It wasn't just you. And have you stopped to think that maybe it wasn't us losing control? Maybe we were just giving in."

"No, I'm not the man for you, Leah. I'm sure your family wants something different for their youngest daughter. Not me. This life isn't what I want for you either."

I slide into his lap before he can stop me. "It doesn't matter what anyone thinks. This is my life. I know what I want," I say in a hushed voice, lips coasting along his. "And I think you want the same thing."

Mikhail's fingers dig into my hips. "Your father and Rod would try to kill me if they knew—"

"Knew what? That I'm in your lap and that you can feel how wet I am for you." I undulate my hips, and his cock hits at the perfect angle as he groans into my neck. "Look at me, Mikhail. I want you to see me."

"Leah..." He presses me against his erection.

Yes, yes...

"Mikhail!" Rodrigo's voice booms from the front door. "'Bout fucking time you show up."

No. No.

Mikhail tosses me back into the passenger seat, adjusting his shirt and the bulge in his pants.

"Fuck."

"Your tints are too dark. He didn't see anything."

"Needs to stay that way."

His tone is harsh, and I have to admit, it stings. The car's cabin is suddenly suffocating, so I push the door open and gaze up in time to see my brother's shocked and confused look as I emerge.

"What the fuck?"

"Found her broke down on the side of the road," Mikhail says, exiting the car a moment later.

"Broke down? What damn car? Leah, what the hell? Why didn't you tell me you were coming?"

I plaster on my innocent little sister smile and spring into his arms. "Rodri, I wanted to surprise you and Papá. But I ended up renting a beater." I twist toward Mikhail and wrap my arms around his middle in a tight hug. He tenses, but fuck that. I hold him tighter. "Mikhail, here, rescued me."

A wave of uncertainty seems to pass over my brother's face as he glances between me and his friend for a beat, then shrugs with a sigh. "Well, fuck. That was lucky."

"Perfect timing," I say, taking deliberately slow steps toward the door. Somehow, I can feel Mikhail's eyes on me.

"What the fuck, Leah? Are those shorts or goddamn denim underwear?"

I release an aggravated groan as I pass through the open door. My agitation is short-lived when I'm bombarded with squeals and hugs from my mom and sister. I wait until my dad is in the room to explain the last several hours so I won't have to tell the same damn story twice.

I twist my wet hair into a bun as the steam from my shower swirls around me and condenses on the mirror. Swiping it with the palm of my hand, I stare at my distorted reflection.

"What am I doing?" I whisper to myself, brushing a finger over my lip where Mikhail's phantom kisses still linger. Pride swells in my chest despite the doubts and slight regret because our friendship will never be the same. I was bold tonight. I went for what I've always wanted. And maybe things didn't turn out exactly as I envisioned, but at least now I know I affected him, and he sees me as a woman and not just that naive little girl from years ago.

A soft knock on the door makes my heart accelerate with excitement until my sister's voice calls for me on the other side. Disappointment has me sulking, but what do I expect? Mikhail?

"Hey. You calling it a night so soon?" my sister asks, letting herself inside.

"It's been a long day."

She plops down on my bed. "Or you bailed when the love of your life walked out the door."

Ann has known about my crush on Mikhail since the night of my *Quince* when he showed up with some whore on his arm who couldn't keep her hands to herself. She found me crying my eyes out under a dark stairwell and refused to leave until I told her why I was upset. I remember being ready to lash out, expecting her to laugh and call me foolish, but I should have known Ann would never. She's different from me and Rodrigo. Such an empath with a tender heart. While her loyalties will always be with her family, regardless of the darkness that shrouds us, I know she craves more out of life.

Better.

Some days, I wish we were more alike. Maybe then, college life would have felt more fulfilling and hopeful, a way to branch out and leave all this behind. But the pull and intrigue of the only life I've known has always had its claws wedged deep into my heart.

"I kissed him, Ann," I say, suddenly emotional. My sister gasps and pulls me into a tight hug.

"It's okay. Maybe his rejection is exactly what you need to move on."

"No...he sat me on his lap and kissed me back."

Her mouth falls open.

"Well, shit."

"Yeah."

"What does this mean, Lee? You know that—"

"I know. But I don't care. *Papá* loves me. He'll understand. And Mikhail is practically part of this family."

Ann huffs a heavy breath. "Leah, you know how things work. He's a Petrov."

I storm to my feet and pace, my steps heavy. "Are we really so different, though?"

My sister catches my arm. "Maybe not"—she looks up at me, her voice softening and her eyes somber—"but in this family, you know your role."

"Bullshit. I'm not marrying some random asshole. I won't be auctioned off like livestock for money. You didn't have to, so why should I?"

She hangs her head, and I instantly feel racked with guilt. In our world, daughters of powerful men are often betrothed to the sons of other powerful families in the hopes of gaining wealth and increasing assets. And not just by combining last names, but by producing heirs. Like Ann, women who can't bear children are free to choose their paths. And frankly, I'm not sure who's the lucky one between us.

"I'm sorry," I say, sitting beside her and throwing an arm around her shoulder. "I wasn't thinking."

"I'm sure it's been quite a night for you." She shoves me back and flashes a slow smile. "How about a movie night? Your pick."

"I'll probably be asleep twenty minutes in, but let's do it."

Ann jumps to her feet. "I'll get the popcorn started," she chirps excitedly and heads for the door. "I'm glad you're home."

The moment it clicks, I pull the towel from my hair and close my eyes as the long, damp tendrils tumble over my shoulders. "Me too," I sigh, letting myself collapse onto the bed

MIKHAIL PETROV 19

CHAPTER THREE
LEAH

The scent of eggs, bacon, and coffee takes me back to childhood. I follow it to the kitchen, where my parents dance to an old-school song I recognize as one from their wedding. It's a *cumbia* that has been on repeat since I was a little girl, especially on Saturday mornings—the only day of the week when life moved slowly, with no obligations, church, school, or work.

It was the one day our family felt normal.

I observe my parents from the doorway, unable to suppress a smile as they twirl and laugh around the island. Their marriage was arranged, of course, but my mother fell madly in love almost immediately. And while what they built is beautiful, it's rare, and I hate that my father tries to use their relationship against me. He'll never understand that my heart is already taken.

"*Mija!* You're up early." My mother giggles when he dips her as the song's last note fades.

"I'm still in another time zone," I lie. In reality, I barely slept. My brain was too busy replaying my kiss with Mikhail.

"Well, fix your breakfast. We're headed out. And wait thirty minutes before you get in the water," she says, eyeing the bikini strap poking out of my oversized t-shirt.

I roll my eyes like a good daughter should and grab a mug from the cabinet. My father leaves without so much as a good morning. He's not speaking to me after I came clean about dropping out of school last night. He didn't say much then either, but something tells me he's already plotting the next steps of my life without my consent—or so he thinks.

The doorbell rings as I pour my coffee, followed by an unexpected voice.

Mikhail.

I toss my cup into the sink and pull my hair out of the messy bun at the top of my head.

"Leah's in the kitchen," I hear my mom say.

He's asking for me.

Drawing in a deep breath, I rest my elbows on the counter…but it pushes my boobs together, and I'm worried it will make me look too desperate.

It's not like you weren't dry humping him in his car or anything.

I switch positions and lean over the back of a stool.

But now I look stupid, like I'm waiting for him.

Fuck.

Dashing toward the fridge, I grab a bowl of blueberries and pop a handful into my mouth.

Shit.

Now, I'll have a mouthful of food when he greets me.

As I try to make a run for the trash bin before he appears at the doorway, I nearly trip over my feet and end up inhaling the fucking berries. I brace a hand on my knee and cover my mouth as I cough violently, trying to expel the fruit from my lungs.

A gentle hand pushes my hair away from my face while the other pats my back.

"Hey, pretty girl, you okay?"

I'm not sure if I want to die of embarrassment, lack of oxygen, or the fact he used my old nickname.

"Breathe," he croons, walking me over to a stool.

My cough finally settles after a few minutes, but by this time, I want to crawl under a rock.

"I'm sorry," I croak as I try to catch my breath.

He chuckles. "You're the one choking. No need to apologize."

Heat rises up my neck and warms my cheeks. God, he must think I'm pathetic. "Death by blueberries, who knew," I joke, trying to play off my humiliation.

"I'm going to have to keep these away from you now."

Mikhail's words make my belly flutter. He's always affected me this way, but something is different. Maybe it's because there's a chance for us. I can feel it.

"What are you doing here so early?"

I need to deflect. I'm still relearning how to breathe, and the way his green eyes are focused on me makes expanding my lungs nearly impossible.

He reaches into his back pocket and pulls out my phone, causing a smile to tilt the corners of my mouth as I lift my gaze back to his. "You went back for my phone?"

"It was on the way." He shrugs.

I shake my head with a grin. "Liar."

There it is. That look, the fire in his eyes. He's never looked at me this way in the past.

Throwing my arms around him, I press my lips to his neck and whisper a thank you, though he quickly dashes my hopes when his hands pry mine away.

"I did some thinking last night. And we kind of got off to a crazy start. I've known you for a while, Leah. We've always been friends. And I don't want that to change."

Is he friend-zoning me? The high I'm riding begins to crash.

Friends?

Fucking. Friends.

I plaster on a fake smile. I can play his game.

"Don't worry, nothing's changed, Mikki," I say, throwing his nickname back at him. "You should stay. Rodri is coming over later. In the meantime, we can hang by the pool. You know, like old times."

With that, I slide off the stool, grazing his body in the process, and pull the t-shirt up over my head. I couldn't have picked a better morning to wear this tiny white bikini. As I stroll to the sliding glass doors leading to the pool, I cast a glance over my shoulder and catch him eye-fucking my ass.

Thong for the win.

MIKHAIL PETROV   25

CHAPTER FOUR
MIKHAIL

Two Weeks Later

The Castellanos' front gate slides open as I drive through for the fourth time this week. I paced my living this morning like a fucking jackass, trying to come up with an excuse to see her. The times I've visited since Rodrigo moved out were limited to special occasions or a rare meeting with Emilio. Justifying my frequent visits these last fourteen days has become a daily challenge. But I can't help myself. The need to see and be around her is far greater than my pride.

So when she texted me this morning to ask for help with moving her things to the suite above the pool house, I couldn't jump in my car fast enough. I'm not sure what's happening, and I'm probably not helping the situation by failing to keep my distance, but the more time I spend with Leah, the harder it is to give a damn.

"Mikhail."

Emilio's tone is curt. He's never been one to offer affection to those outside of his circle, so it doesn't come as a surprise. But there's an extra bite to the way he grits out my name. And I don't miss the tension in his shoulders as he stands in the doorway, like a blockade. While we've been associates for eight years, our relationship is brittle and based solely on mutual ambition and power.

"Emilio," I reply with a nod.

"I'd say it's a surprise to see you here *again*, but I'm almost starting to expect your car pulling into my drive more than not."

"Leah asked me to help with the move." I lean on the door frame and fold my arms.

"Of course she did," he replies, narrowing his eyes and glancing around the foyer. "Look, I'm not stupid. I don't like to be taken as a fool. I don't know your intentions, but I suggest you rethink what you're getting yourself into."

I rub a hand over my chin, unable to hide the smirk stretching across my face. The unspoken threat behind his words is loud and clear, but surely, he forgets who he's speaking to. I'm a fucking Petrov, and men lose their heads for smaller acts of disrespect.

"I'm not sure what you're talking about," I say, calling his bluff.

He scoffs. "Leah is not for you, Mikhail. I won't say it twice because the day I let my youngest daughter be turned into a whore by some Russian scum, it will be over my dead body."

I clench my fists. He doesn't realize how quickly that can be arranged.

"Is that right?"

A devious grin splits his face. "I have plans for her. Men worthy of a queen."

My chest tightens as every cell in my body revolts against the idea of another man touching what's mine.

Mine.

It hits me with the force of a nuclear explosion.

Leah is mine.

The affection I've always held for her has shifted into something more these past few weeks. Maybe from the moment I picked her up off that goddamn highway.

Like an act of fucking fate.

"I heard through the grapevine that your father has similar plans for you. Celeste, is it?"

Ice chills my veins at the mention of her name, and I suck in a breath, stepping forward and feeling reckless, but another voice eases the suffocating tension.

"Mikhail, come on! The pizza is getting cold." Leah takes my wrist and tugs me inside.

As I pass, Emilio and I stare each other down as silent threats spark between us.

"Was I interrupting something?" she asks, looking over her shoulder before climbing the staircase to the suite.

I shake my head. "Nah. Your father and I were just discussing business."

Leah's eyebrows pinch slightly as she studies my face, but her skepticism fades when I pluck a small feather from her bun.

"Ann was here this morning, and I kind of started a pillow fight," she explains, cheeks flushing pink.

It's as if I'm seeing her with new eyes, and she's fucking adorable, but in a way that makes me want to kiss her, hold her, and fold her over the side of the couch.

"Ready to get your hands dirty?"

Her question is unintentionally loaded with sexual innuendos, and my cock understands every single one.

"Always," I reply, my gaze locked on hers as heat simmers between us. I know she feels it.

"Good. But first, pizza. I'm starving." Leah flips open the cardboard lid, and my smile evaporates the moment I see our lunch.

"They ran out of pepperoni?"

"Don't tell me you're one of those people who hate pineapple and ham for no reason."

I bark a laugh. "Don't tell me *you* are one of those who actually like this shit."

She picks up a slice and pops a small wedge of the blasphemous fruit into her mouth. "Mmm," she moans, eyes closed. "My favorite."

Maybe the damn thing isn't so bad. If she makes that noise for me with every bite, it'll also be my new favorite.

"I'm not convinced yet," I say. "Take another bite."

Leah nibbles on her lip, smoky eyes on my mouth as she brings the slice closer. "You try it," she urges, breaking off a piece.

Holding her hand, I bring it into my mouth and kiss the tip of her finger.

"What are you doing, *friend?*" Her voice is breathy, her chest rising and falling a little bit faster.

"Tasting the worst fucking pizza I've ever had."

We break into sudden peals of laughter as I spit the bite of pizza into a napkin.

"You are such a pussy, Mikki."

That word falling from her lips quells my laughter and, like it's the most natural thing to do, I wind my arm around her waist and pull her to my chest.

"You have a dirty mouth, pretty girl."

"Mikhail?" she questions, eyes pinging back and forth, unaware I've decided to keep her.

"What is it, *moya krasavitsa?*" Her eyes drift closed as I grip her chin and slant my lips over hers.

"Please don't hurt me, Mikhail."

I know what that means. Two weeks ago, I proposed we simply remain friends. And since then, even with our proximity, I've been careful to keep her at a distance, guarding her heart. But I know now, I've just been protecting my own.

"I'd die before hurting you."

Her smile widens against my lips, body wrapping around mine as I lift her into my arms and kiss her like it's the first time. Yet even as I'm drowning in her essence, I can't help but think how our union can destroy everything I've built for the last eight years. The thought is a sobering one, but not enough to tear me away.

"Leah!" Rodrigo calls from the bottom of the stairs, though neither of us moves with urgency, too reluctant to let the other go.

"He's coming," she squeaks.

I finally let her slide down my body, grazing my aching cock.

"Come back to my place later so we can talk."

She nods lazily, moving to a stool at the breakfast bar just as Rod appears in the doorway.

"I still can't believe you let Mom guilt you into staying here," he says, eyeing us briefly before making a beeline to the pizza. "Aw, fuck, Leah. You still eat this shit?"

CHAPTER FIVE
MIKHAIL

I peer over the checkout line, searching for Leah. The hardware store is surprisingly packed, even thirty minutes from closing. On our way back to my place, she insisted we stop and pick up supplies for tomorrow.

Another glance at my watch confirms she's been gone too long for what the item she was searching for requires. I try not to jump to conclusions but don't take chances regarding people I care for. Stepping out of line, I pull out my phone and punch in her contact as groans rise from the customers behind me.

Fuck them.

I stalk toward the back of the store where she's supposed to be, but there's no one there but a petite woman stocking some items on a shelf. Leah's voicemail adds to my growing anxiety.

"Did you see a young woman back here? Long, dark hair. About 5'5". White shorts. Black top."

The lady straightens, and her eyebrows crinkle as if recalling the memory.

"Oh, yeah. Pretty girl wearing Converse. Javier took her out back.

Said something about extra stock on some palettes."

A sinking feeling in the pit of my stomach steals my breath as I race toward a set of double doors that leads me down a short corridor before opening into an empty back lot. It's dark, with just a dim light blinking in the distance.

I cup my mouth, ready to belt out her name, until I hear her voice.

"Don't touch me. What the fuck is wrong with you?"

My feet move before the action even becomes a thought.

"Fuck you. You ain't that pretty anyway." A man's scathing voice follows.

Oh, this type of fun wasn't on my plans for tonight, but I'll gladly add it.

"I said don't touch me." A low thud echoes from around the corner, immediately followed by the man's roar of expletives.

In the next instant, Leah crashes into my arms. It takes another few seconds for her to realize I'm not a threat.

"Shit!" she squeaks, out of breath from nerves and the short sprint.

"Are you okay?"

She nods. "That asshole. I don't know what he thought was going to happen, but—"

"Go to the car," I say, cutting her off and looking beyond her.

"Mikhail, let's just go."

Before I can argue, the bastard in question rounds the corner, blood gushing from the middle of his face. Scooting Leah behind me, I pull a blade from my pocket and approach a dead man walking. He must see the bloodlust written on my face because his eyes blow wide, and he puts his hands up in defense.

"Hey, I didn't—"

I bury the knife in his stomach and shred across his flesh until he's howling in my ear like a little bitch. Without a moment of reprieve, I fist his uniform vest and drag him toward a chain-link fence where cables of barbed wire lay on the ground.

"Fuck, man…I'm sorry, I didn't know she was your girl… Just wanted her number." Voice strangled, his arms hug his middle in a frantic fight to keep his intestines from flopping out of his body.

"Today is not a good day for you."

The edges of sharp blades pierce my skin as I wind the wire around his neck. Three, four, five times, squeezing harder with every twist until it's embedded deep into his throat, and he's no longer moving.

When I turn around, Leah stands still, eyes fixed on me. I can't tell if she's breathing or blinking.

"Did he hurt you?" My blood stains her skin when I frame her face.

Her head moves from side to side as if in slow motion. Pain cuts through me, and my chest grows heavy with anguish at her silence.

Is she in shock? Disgusted by the fact I can brutally kill another man in cold blood.

For her.

But a heartbeat later, she's in my arms, lips crushed against mine. And that's when I know my life has a purpose.

My phone vibrates with a message, confirming that my clean-up crew has cleared the scene and removed Javier's body.

I tighten the towel around my waist as I move through my kitchen, chugging a bottle of water, when the doorbell rings, catching me off guard. When I pull up the footage on my phone, I see Leah standing at my front entrance, nervously tucking loose strands of hair behind her ear.

"Why didn't you tell me you were coming? I would have picked you up or been on alert. It's late."

"I'm sorry. I couldn't sleep. I needed to see you."

I pull her into a tight hug. "What's on your mind, pretty girl?"

She looks up at me and offers a frail smile. "I need to know if this is real. You killed for me, Mikhail. And I want you to know that I would kill for you, too."

"I'd never ask you to do that."

Leah backs out of my arms and lifts her shirt above her head. "You wouldn't have to."

She isn't wearing a bra, and when she drops her sweatpants, I learn she left her panties at home as well. My eyes rake over every beautiful inch of her.

"Are you sure?" I ask, dropping kisses onto her shoulder.

"I wouldn't be naked in your living room if I wasn't."

Leah is nineteen. I'm twenty-seven. While she's a full-fledged adult, there are still eight years between us and our experiences.

"I'm not a virgin, Mikhail. You don't need to be gentle or feel weird," she assures me, possibly sensing my hesitancy.

"Who do I need to kill?" I chuckle against her lips.

Leah remains silent, a severe expression creasing her brow despite my joke. "I already killed him."

I won't lie; her confession shocks me for a moment. But I'm curious more than anything.

"I'm listening."

She huffs a breath and averts her gaze. "He took a video without my consent. And he threatened to post it online and make it go viral if I didn't sleep with his friends and whoever else was willing to pay. He deserved it, Mikhail. And I don't regret it."

If he weren't already dead, I'd be booking a flight to New York.

Lifting her chin, I bring her gaze back to mine and smile. "Good girl."

It's all the reassurance she needs. Leah unties the towel at my waist and strokes my cock. "I always knew your dick was perfect. It's going to hurt like a bitch, but I'm up for the challenge."

She drops to her knees and takes me into her mouth. Slow licks and sucks at first until it's wet enough for her to slide to the back of her throat as far as she can.

"Fuck," I growl, closing my eyes and gripping her bun in a fist. I slam her down until she gags and pulls back, taking a short breath before she swallows me again. "My pretty girl, look at you, taking my cock so goddamn deep, like it was made for your throat."

Leah grips my ass and pushes to the limit as tears streak down her cheeks.

"Oh, hell…*Prosto tak. Ty tak khorosho menya prinimayesh', krasavitsa..*" (Just like that. You're taking me so good, beautiful.)

My balls coil the harder I pump into her warm mouth. But as much as I want to see my cum dripping from those skilled lips, the need to be inside her wins out. Pulling back, my cock pops out of her mouth, and she looks up at me like a goddess.

"Come here," I say as I take her hand and help her up, then step behind her as I loosen her hair until it tumbles down her back. "I want you to know that I never thought of you this way before now. And I don't regret that."

"I know," she whispers, tilting her head as I run my lips against the curve of her neck.

"But you're mine now."

"I know," she says again, voice breaking on a whimper as I slide my fingers between the seam of her wet little cunt.

"All this for me." I walk us to the couch and sit with her in my lap, thighs spread wide over mine, and my cock at her entrance. "Take your time," I murmur into her ear as she slides down my shaft.

"Mikhail...*fuck*," she moans and lets her head fall back onto my shoulder as I stretch her open, inch by inch. Her chest is heaving, mouth parted when I bottom out and grip her hips.

"Ride what's yours, baby. You take care of me, and I take care of you." Reaching around her pelvis, I find her swollen clit and stroke until she's crying in my lap. "*Krasivaya devushka*, you were made for me. This sweet pussy was made for me." (Pretty girl.)

"I know..." she repeats for the third time, and I can't help but laugh.

We're riding a high together, finding the perfect rhythm as I thrust and she bounces.

The moment is surreal as we tip over the edge, and I hold her tightly against my chest. Coming home has a new meaning as the sound of my name flees her lips when she breaks.

MIKHAIL PETROV   39

CHAPTER SIX
LEAH

Two weeks later

"Hold it, please!"

I sprint toward the elevator as fast as I can manage with a tray of two milkshakes and a bag of the best greasy burgers in Dallas. A guy who looks to be my age does me a solid and slips his foot through the closing doors, forcing them back open.

"Thank you," I say with a smile.

"Sure thing. Bringing the boss some lunch?"

"Something like that." I'm also bringing dessert, but he doesn't need to know that it's in the form of me living out an office fantasy on my knees and behind the boss's desk.

It's been two weeks of utter bliss with Mikhail. We've kept our relationship under wraps for obvious reasons, but eventually, our families will have to accept that we belong together. I'm tired of lying and sneaking around. I'm too old for this bullshit, and so is he.

When the elevator doors slide open, I exit and smile at the kind stranger on my way out. A redhead with the brightest blue eyes I've ever seen sits behind a desk. She side-eyes my heels and pencil skirt, then lifts her gaze to my low-cut blouse, probably wondering whether I'm an employee even though we've never met.

"Name?" she asks, without so much as a greeting.

Rude.

"I'm here to see Mikhail Petrov."

She arches an eyebrow and feigns an apologetic smile. "I'm sorry, but Mr. Petrov has no visitors on his schedule today."

"That's okay." I shrug.

"No, you don't understand. He can't see you if you don't have an appointment."

"I don't need one, Heather. When I rolled out of his bed this morning, I told him I'd be by for lunch."

Now those eyebrows nearly hit her hairline. "I'll let him know you're here."

I flash her my most cynical smile and continue down the hall. "No need. I can find it."

As I near Mikhail's office door, I can see it's cracked open, and a woman's voice is coming from a speaker. I don't want to eavesdrop, but her tone has a strange undercurrent of familiarity, and the things she's saying don't add up.

"Your father lined everything out in the contract, including the mergers and assets. He said he'd talk to you, but since you haven't called, I figured I'd reach out."

"I've been busy."

There's a stretch of silence before she responds.

"Mikhail, the original date for our wedding is in a month. I won't wait any longer than that. My father has…*other* prospects. I expect an answer by this weekend."

The room suddenly feels like a vacuum, sucking all the air from my lungs.

"Celeste," he says through clenched teeth.

"The ball is in your court. Goodbye, Mikhail."

I hear my boyfriend sigh like the world's weight is on his shoulders. Although I'm sure juggling a girlfriend and a fiancée will do that to a man—or rather, a cheating sack of shit.

I take a moment and swallow the crippling pain of betrayal before bursting through the door.

"You better not keep her waiting." No matter how much I try to hold back my traitorous tears, they come flooding forward.

Mikhail jumps to his feet and tries to approach me, but I step back and shake my head. "Don't fucking touch me."

"Baby, it's not what you think."

I slam the bag of food on the floor. "Oh, I'm sorry; please tell me how you having a fiancée is somehow a miscommunication on my part."

He reaches for me again, but I recoil, threatening to toss milkshakes all over his expensive suit. "Leah, Celeste is not my fiancée in the way you think. I've never met her, and this was our second time speaking. She's business. That's all. And this was before you."

I squeeze my eyes closed. "I told you not to hurt me. Please, don't lie to me."

"I'm not lying," he says, taking the milkshake tray from my shaky hands and placing it on his desk. I feel the warmth of his presence just inches from me and his lips on my forehead.

"So why not tell her the wedding is off?" I open my eyes when there's no answer and look up at his weary expression. "Mikhail?"

He rakes a rough hand across his face. "Things aren't that simple."

Again, I feel the gut punch. "What do you mean?" No answer. My heart thumps in my throat. "Mikhail, answer me right this moment. Are you going to marry her or not?"

"Leah, fuck— I thought… I have obligations to fulfill. I haven't been thinking straight." My mouth falls open. "If I don't go through with this, not only do I fail my father, but I implicate you with yours, my family."

I shake my head in complete disbelief. "You bastard."

"Leah, please. This kills me."

"You weren't too torn up this morning when you had me on my knees in the shower or last night when you fucked me on the kitchen counter— Oh no, you weren't worried then." I slap his hand away when he tilts my chin.

"Because I wasn't," he grits out. "But it's like the whole goddamn world started burning around me on the same day. Your father all but threatened me and my family because he suspects something is going on between us. He showed up this morning, surrounded by his lackeys, trying to intimidate me. Then my father pressuring me with this Celeste bullshit. Of course, he tells me it's my choice, but I know what he expects at the end of the day."

Mikhail knocks over a stack of documents and pounds his desk. Maybe it's naive and stupid of me to feel for him. But I understand the pressures he's facing. I'm in similar shoes.

I place a hand on his back. "Mikhail," I nearly whisper. He whirls around in a flash and scoops me into his arms.

"Celeste means nothing. I need you to believe that, pretty girl."

"You should have told me."

He nods and cups my face. "I should have, and I'm sorry."

"Let's leave, Mikhail. You and me. Somewhere, anywhere, away from all of this."

He sighs. "Leah…you know we can't do that."

"Don't do it, Mikhail. Don't marry her." I grip his wrists and find his gaze through my tears.

"*Moya krasavitsa*, I want nothing more than to give you what you want…"

I bite my lip to keep it from trembling, but nothing can stop my heart from breaking into unrecognizable shreds.

"Goodbye, Mikhail."

The hallway seems endless as I trudge toward the elevator. I catch Heather in my peripheral, her scrutinizing eyes following me until I slide inside and slink to the back corner. Once the doors close, I allow my tears to fall freely and a sob to break from my lips.

He said he wouldn't hurt me.

Liar.

CHAPTER SEVEN
MIKHAIL

Present Day

Fuck.

I huff an exasperated breath and squeeze my eyes shut as my father's voice grates on my last nerve. I love the man, but goddamn. Have I been such a recluse lately that he can't take me at my word that I'll be at the fucking reunion like I am every damn year?

Setting my cell phone on my lap, I rest my head on the seat, calling on my last ounce of patience.

"Rodrigo's guy and I should be done days before then. I'll be there."

Satisfied with my answer, he says his goodbyes, and I close my eyes again, aggravated as all hell on multiple fronts since Rod's call last night telling me he couldn't make our Seattle drop. I stopped listening once he mentioned needing surgery and was sending another bastard in his place. We've been running arms deals for twelve years. I don't trust anyone else to have my back; now, he's forcing my hand. This deal is too important, and there is too much money at stake for me to back out. I'll suck it up, get paid, and be home in two days.

"Mr. Petrov, shall I pull over here or on the tarmac?"

"Pull up, William," I instruct, glancing at my watch. My driver nods. His aged blue eyes find mine in the rearview mirror and crease with a gentle smile.

I arrive forty-five minutes earlier than our scheduled meet-up, needing to size this fucker up before a face-to-face. My phone buzzes as I relax into the sleek leather, Viktor's name lighting up the screen.

Viktor: Heard you got a new partner. Watch your back, bro.

It hasn't been ten minutes since my father's call, and already he's run his mouth. Always fiercely protective, especially since Mom's death. While often aggravating, I understand his paranoia. Our line of work has its risks: death or prison.

"Sir, looks like we have company incoming."

I lock eyes with the approaching SUV and push open my door.

An older man climbs out of the driver's seat and heads toward the trunk to unload his client's bags.

A moment later, the back passenger door swings open, and black boots hit the concrete. They're connected to toned legs and thighs encased in sheer black tights. As my gaze sweeps her figure, a smile moves across my face, and emotions, long bottled up, rush to the surface.

Leah.

"Hi, Mikhail."

I almost feel the need to pinch myself. The woman I fell hard for and lost four years ago stands before me, looking more beautiful and confident than I remember.

"Leah? What—what are you doing here?" Did I stammer? When have I ever stuttered?

Her mouth twitches at my words but slides back into a smile before nodding.

"Surprise."

We didn't exactly end on the best of terms, but I embrace her regardless, and it's almost like time suspends, like she and I have been waiting for this moment since that godforsaken day in my office. As always, she feels so perfect in my arms.

"It's been a while."

"It has."

When the moment passes, she steps back, but her smile doesn't falter. I've always wondered if she resents me for how things ended. But as I gaze into her bright eyes, maybe there's a chance that we can someday rekindle our friendship. A voice at the back of my head screams how friendship will never be enough.

"It's good to see you, Leah."

She gifts me another beaming smile. "Same."

There's a strange charge in the air as we stare at each other silently. There are so many unsettled emotions and words between us. But this isn't the time to hash out the past.

I peer past her and into the vehicle, searching for Rod's guy.

"You come to see us off?" I ask, still focused on the car.

"Not exactly."

"What does that mean?" She has my full attention now.

"It means it's just me."

I digest her statement, jaw ticking as she slings a bag over her shoulder and closes the car door.

"Wait. What do you mean, it's just you? You for what?"

"I'm your guy—your girl. Rodrigo sent me—"

"Stop," I say, blinking furiously and wholly taken back. "You're not implying what I think you are, are you? That you are running this shipment with me?"

"That's exactly what I'm saying."

No. Fuck, no. This has to be a joke. Rodrigo wouldn't screw me over like this, sending his baby sister to an arms deal across the country.

"No, absolutely not."

Leah's face tightens, and she narrows her eyes. "What, you think because I'm a woman, I can't possibly know what the fuck I'm doing? That I'm not good enough?"

"Since when do you run shipments, Leah?"

She gasps and storms up to me, craning her neck to look me in the eye as a perfectly manicured finger points at my face. "Since four years ago when someone screwed me over, so I decided to be spontaneous and join the family business."

"No, the answer is no."

A grin tilts the side of her mouth.

"Well, suit yourself. We're on schedule for the drop, so you either get on the plane or I leave without you. Don't fuck with my money, Mikki."

She claps my chest as she walks past me, then waves over her driver, who's waiting with a black suitcase in hand. A growl rattles in my chest.

She's crazy if she thinks this drop is happening. "Leah, wait."

But she purposely ignores me and disappears into the cabin. I'll kill him. Rodrigo is dead.

"Shall I load your bag, Mr. Petrov?"

I grab the handle of my suitcase and nod at William before making my way up the stairs and onto the private jet. My breath catches in my throat when I find Leah, arms above her head, pulling off her sweater, a delicious sliver of skin on display for me. I've spent the better half of four years trying but failing to forget her, and here she is, making me realize that nothing has changed. The embers she left smoldering in my heart have reignited.

"Leah," I sigh, clearing my head, "this can't happen. You— This is life or death."

"Doesn't that sound familiar?"

She sits on one of the beige leather seats, crossing her legs slowly, capturing my attention. A jolt to the dick makes me shift my weight.

"You know what I mean." Aggravation replaces the nostalgia of her presence.

"Oh, you think my brother just sent his poor, defenseless baby sis to an arms deal for shits and giggles. Did it ever occur to you that this is what I do?"

My forehead creases with intrigue and confusion. "No, last I heard, you moved to Spain."

Hurt flashes in her eyes.

"You think I've just been gallivanting across the globe, spending Daddy's money and looking pretty?"

"I could think of one hundred things you've been doing besides this."

"You're impossible," she groans and gets to her feet. As much as I try to ignore that sweet sound, I instantly crave to hear it again, to hear her break with my name on her lips like she did when she was mine.

"Mikhail, I know what I'm doing."

Leah is standing about a foot in front of me, and the urge to reach for her is damn near overwhelming. But this is business. I can't let our past get in the way of the job.

"Do you?"

She smirks, peering at me through thick lashes, hands crawling up my chest. "Maybe you can be the judge of that?"

I swallow hard and catch her wrists. "That's not what I was referring to."

When she bites her lip, it takes everything in me not to haul her to my waist. "I know what you meant." Freeing herself from my grasp, she struts back to her seat. My eyes stray to her plump little ass beneath a tight grey skirt.

Leah is sin incarnate. I want nothing more than to bend her over the seat, push that goddamn skirt over her ass, and take back what's mine.

MIKHAIL PETROV   53

CHAPTER EIGHT
LEAH

Yesterday, four years felt like an eternity—more than enough time to flush Mikhail Petrov from my system in all the ways I needed him to be gone. Yet all it took was seeing him exit that car for every memory, every kiss, and every caress to come barreling to the surface.

But the worst was how I felt my heart shatter all over again, like I was that nineteen-year-old girl in his office, feeling like the world was caving in on her.

With a deep breath, I steel my resolve. He won't shake me. I didn't come all this way for nothing. Rekindling my relationship with Mikhail is not the reason I'm here. My objective is closure. I've tried to seal this door for years, but somehow, it creeps back open when I least expect it. And I can't move on until all our cards are on the table. Sure, it's an unconventional way to force a conversation, but when has anything about us been practical?

Sneaking a glance, I notice his rigid posture and the crinkle in his eyebrows, and it's clear he's upset and uncomfortable. I don't blame him. He's always been such a stickler when it comes to the family business, and my being here is throwing off his entire game plan. But maybe I don't care.

I shift in my seat, and he tenses.

"Look, I'm sorry." His emerald-green eyes find mine as he waits for me to continue. "I should have let Rod tell you I'd be taking his place. But I swore him to secrecy and threatened to cut off his balls."

The hint of a smile touches his lips. "Why go through all that trouble?"

"Because you know as well as I do you wouldn't have agreed to have me."

"You're right. We could have met under any other circumstance if that's what you wanted. Leah, *how* did you get wrapped up in this?" He leans on the armrest, and his sinful cologne washes over me. "So many unnecessary risks. You deserve better."

My eyes damn near roll to the back of my head. This is the energy I need to sear the half of my heart stuck in the past. "You know what I deserve, Mikhail? To stop being told by the men in my life what I should and shouldn't do. What's good for me and what's not. *That's* why I'm here."

"So you're doing this just to prove some point?"

I dig my fingers into the armrests and push to my feet as a flush of anger rises up my neck. "Yeah, the one that flew right over your thick, stubborn head."

"Where are you going? The seatbelt sign is still on."

"Case in point. I didn't know I needed permission to take a piss."

I click the bathroom lock in place hard enough to nearly break it, then brace my hands on the small sink.

"Channel it, Leah," I say to myself in a whisper as regret roils in the pit of my stomach when I realize he still has power over me...but even worse, that I may still love him. I suddenly question my motives, not the ones I've convinced myself are true, but those buried in the darkest recesses of my mind, locked away to keep my heart safe. I've tried so hard to hate him over the years because, in his eyes, I wasn't worth fighting for. And when I left, I swore I would never see him again. But the moment the opportunity arose, I jumped.

What am I doing here?

I pull out my phone and punch in a message to Ann, hoping the Wi-Fi connection on this damn plane works.

ME: You were right.

Text bubbles appear and disappear before a message finally pops up.

ANN: Are you okay?
ME: I'm stupid.
ANN: Come home.
ME: I can't. I have to see this through.

More text bubbles come and go before the next message pops up.

ANN: Guard your heart. You're worth it. I love you.

Placing my phone on the ledge, I drag in a breath and compose myself, dabbing at an insolent tear beading at the corner of my eye. Two days. I have two days to clear the air and move on…or…

Or what?

Mikhail ends a call the moment he sees me emerge from the bathroom. Curiosity has me narrowing my eyes, but I decide not to question him.

"I'm sorry," he blurts, almost too fast to understand. And I suddenly wonder what he's apologizing for. "Leah, it's been a while, and even though things ended on rocky terms, I am glad to see you."

The way his voice softens, his eyes lingering and dropping to my lips when he doesn't think I notice, only blows the damn door open even wider.

"It's good to see you too."

"Can I ask you something? But only if you promise not to get upset."

I scoff and relax in my seat. "People only lead with that when they know they're about to ask a triggering question. But go on."

Why he feels the need to creep closer is beyond me, but I hate that I very much don't hate his proximity.

"How did you convince Rod to let you do this? And does your father know?"

I match his boldness and place my forearms on the armrest, inches from him, knowing damn well he has a clear view down my cami. "My father thinks I'm still in Spain. And as for Rodri, you'd be surprised what a man will agree to under the influence of narcotics."

He moves closer still, this time not trying to hide that his eyes are focused on my lips, and when I wet them, he draws a hard breath in through his nose. "Why? Why are you here?"

Mikhail's harsh voice doesn't match his body language. All the vulnerable pieces of him I once knew are unraveling before me, and I don't think he realizes it. He's ruthless and cold to the world, but with me, he's always been soft and patient.

"You don't want me?" The words tumble out, and I want to regret them because this isn't what I came here for, but with my pride slowly leaving the plane, maybe I'm changing my mind.

"Leah—"

"Sir, would you and the lady like a drink?" The young man in black uniform is part of the flight crew. He offers me a friendly smile, but it fades when his eyes fall on Mikhail, who's now upright against his seat, eyes plastered forward.

"No," he says, almost from between his teeth.

"And you, miss?"

I'm suddenly intrigued by Mikhail's behavior and decide to test the waters.

"I'm Leah," I respond, even though he doesn't exactly ask. "And you are?"

"Benjamin, or Benny." His shoulders loosen, smile brightening, and I don't miss the sweeping glance he gives me.

"Benny, how about you show me what you got? Is that okay?"

He nods enthusiastically, akin to a golden retriever. Mikhail remains still, except for the tension on his face he seems to be trying to temper with shallow breaths.

Rising to my feet, I cross in front of him, and his arm suddenly shoots out and grips my wrist.

"Sit down, Leah."

Fuck. Me.

The command sends a spark racing down my spine like a live wire connected to my pussy. My knees are suddenly wobbly. So help me, I'll do anything he asks.

Taking two strides backward, my legs hit the seat, and I plop down.

"Benjamin," he says, tone razor sharp, "the lady will take water. You're dismissed."

I feel bad for poor Benny. His cheeks are flaming red. And he avoids my gaze as he nods before quickly disappearing behind us.

"He was about to piss himself. Why so rude, Mikki?"

Mikhail's glare slides over to me. "What are you doing?"

"What's your problem? I think I can handle walking ten feet with your employee and choosing a drink. And water? Really?"

"You were flirting with him. We're here on business, not to pick up the staff."

Jealousy.

"I don't flirt. And even if I was, why would that bother you?"

"Leah."

"Answer the question, Mikhail."

"Because I feel responsible for you."

I chuckle dryly. "Responsible for me? That's your answer?"

He leans over the armrest again, his expression all hard lines made of ice. "Were you expecting something different?"

"No, unfortunately." His jaw twitches at my remark. "But we're a team. And that's where it ends because what I do, who I flirt with— who I *fuck*—is my business."

Mikhail looks away from me and drags a hand across his beard. "This is going to be the longest goddamn flight of my life."

CHAPTER NINE
MIKHAIL

Leah hasn't said another word in over an hour. And I've purposely kept my distance. I know she's upset, but what does she expect? She shows up here after four years just to fuck with me and turn everything on its head. This morning, I would have said I was in a better place regarding the girl I had to let go…because it's how things needed to be.

How they need to stay.

But now… *Now,* my hands buzz with the need to touch her. To pull her into my lap, keep her, and make her mine.

"Sir." Benjamin's voice is like goddamn nails on a chalkboard. I suppress the urge to wrap my hand around his scrawny little throat and choke the fucking life from his eyes. The balls on this bastard.

Without looking his way, I motion with my hand for him to get to the point.

"Captain says we're going to hit some turbulence. There's a storm ahead."

Seconds crawl by, and he, for whatever reason, remains standing in place.

"Thanks, Benny." Leah breaks her streak of silence. For fucking

Benjamin, no less. "You don't have to treat him like that. He didn't do anything wrong," she says once he retreats.

"I'm not here to make friends. He did his job and doesn't need a pat on the back."

I click my seatbelt and wait for Leah to do the same. But she resumes her silence, gazing out the window. I bite my tongue, knowing damn well if I mention it, that will just be another reason for us to argue, something we never did in the past. And I hate it.

But when the first jolts of turbulence rock the plane enough that she slips from one side of her seat to the other, I can't hold back any longer.

"Seatbelt, Leah."

She doesn't lash out. Instead, she fidgets as if searching for something. "Shit, my phone. I must have left it in the bathroom."

Jumping to her feet, she makes a run for it, but is quickly tossed backward by another heavy jostle of the plane. I snap off my seatbelt and lunge, catching her before she's thrown to the ground. Unfortunately, my back rams into the edge of a seat, partially knocking the air from my lungs.

"Oh my god, Mikhail. Are you okay?"

"Fuck," I groan at the pain, but as long as she isn't hurt, then it's well worth the bruising or cracked rib. "I'm good."

Leah attempts to break out of my arms, but I hold firm and push to my feet while cradling her. We manage to make it to my chair without incident, and I stretch the belt to accommodate her body over my lap.

"I'm sorry. But you shouldn't have done that. What if you cracked your head instead? And Mikhail…why am I in your lap?"

"But I didn't. And you're here because you're stubborn, and I don't want you running off again and getting hurt." I wonder if she can hear how fast my heart is thundering. It's like a steady bass in my chest.

"Lesson learned," she murmurs as I tuck hair behind her ear.

"Better safe than sorry." My thumb brushes her chin, then moves over her lip, and God, I want to fucking kiss her. *"Takaya upryamaya i takaya krasivaya."* (So stubborn and so beautiful.)

Leah's lashes flutter as she leans into my touch. *"Ya bol'she ne tvoya krasavitsa?"* (Am I not your pretty girl anymore?)

My eyes snap up to meet hers. "You learned Russian?"

"Da."

My cheeks are on fire, and I realize it's from smiling so goddamn much. "What made you want to do that?"

She shrugs. "I was bored, and I figured if I ever saw you again, what better way to get revenge than to curse you out in your own language."

I tip my head and laugh. "Touche. And I probably deserve it."

"Probably."

A vortex of emotions rage through me. I know I should let her go in more ways than just this moment, but I can't bring myself to do it. Not yet.

"It's probably safer if I sit in my seat," she says, reaching for the latch.

But I catch her hand and shake my head. "You're always safe with me—and I can't risk it. I'm fresh out of partners at the moment."

She closes her eyes and draws a breath. "I've missed you."

"Leah…"

"I don't want you to think that I came here to try to rekindle what we had. I came for closure, Mikhail. Because your memory still haunts me." I wipe a tear from the corner of her lips. "We used to talk every day. You were my best friend. And then, one day, you were just gone. So I had to leave."

The unresolved pain in her eyes lances through me, fresh and raw like the day we said goodbye.

"Fuck, Leah…I never wanted to hurt you. But I felt like my hands were tied," I say, cupping her face.

"You let my dad, my brother, your family…tear us apart. I wanted to be enough and for you *to see me*."

I rest my forehead on her chest and grip her hips. "*Krasivaya devushka*, (Pretty girl.) I do. Fuck, I do. That's what you don't understand. You're all I've seen for a long time."

A small gasp falls from her lips, and before I can stop myself, I'm kissing her like I haven't been able to in four fucking years. I draw her closer, and it's still not enough.

"I need you to be quiet for me. Can you do that?"

Leah whimpers into my mouth when I squeeze her thigh and slowly ascend until I find the edge of the tights around her waist. I yank the frail fabric and the strap of her thong until they give.

"I've missed this, pretty girl," I say, sliding my fingers along her slick opening. She clutches my collar and bites down on my neck when my knuckle circles her clit.

"Me too."

I tear at the seatbelt's latch and reposition her so that she's straddling my lap, then dive back into her sweet cunt without wasting another second.

"You'll have to be quieter than that." Bringing my wet fingers to her lips, I shove them inside and slip them against her tongue. Leah moans, hollowing her pretty mouth until she gags. "Benny has one strike left, and if he so much as breathes this way, I'll gouge out his eyes."

She shakes her head, moaning around my fingers.

"That's my girl." The loss of my touch has her rocking her hips against my thigh. "It's been so goddamn long since I've seen you fall apart for me."

I slip from her mouth, grab the hem of her blouse, and tear it over her head. The plane suddenly jerks, and I hurriedly throw an arm around her while the other grips the seat, keeping us in place.

"You okay?" I ask, pressing my lips to the bridge of her nose where her skin is tinged pink.

"I will be once you put your hands on my pussy again."

Chuckling along the column of her neck, I trail kisses lower until my face is buried in her breasts.

"Touch me, Mikhail," she begs, rubbing her cunt on my pant leg.

I reach around her ass and drag two fingers over her slit.

"I want you to ruin my pants, pretty girl. Like you ruined me."

The world outside this plane doesn't exist. Not when we're 30,000 feet in the air. Nothing matters beyond this woman grinding against my cock and crying my name.

"Fuck, Mikhail…I'm coming."

"Yes…that's it," I urge as I grab her throat, wholly enraptured by her beautiful face as she splinters.

Warm, wet, and throbbing against me, Leah has me aching for my own release, to sink inside her until we're both utterly useless.

"My turn," she says with a grin and slinks to the floor on her knees, freeing my cock from the aching confines of these goddamn pants.

When her mouth slides down my shift, I curl a fist into her hair and tip my head back against the seat.

How have I lived four years without her?

"Mikhail, I know this goes without saying, but watch out for her. You know she's a little crazy, and I'm pretty sure she fucking drugged me. If my dad finds out she's with you, he'll put my head on a spike."

I don't answer. Reality coming to collect.

"Hey, did you hear me?" Rodrigo's voice rattles in my ear.

"Yeah, don't worry. I'll get her home."

I stare at the dark phone screen long after hanging up. My thoughts are in disarray.

As I watch her sleeping form, the pit of my stomach hollows. I can't pinpoint the emotion festering inside me.

"Hey…" Her voice is thick with sleep as she sits up and stretches before touching my arm. I thought I told you not to let me fall asleep." She pulls my knuckle to her lips and presses a kiss. But the longer our eyes connect, the more she realizes something has fractured. Her beautiful smile fades when I don't offer one in return.

"What's wrong?" she asks.

Slipping my hand from hers, I adjust my body, and with a slight shake of my head, I say, "Leah, this can't happen."

Silence chills the air between us. I wait for her to process, to say something, anything, but she remains quiet.

"The alliance between my family and yours is too important. Everything we've built over the years…my future—I can't just throw that away for…"

"For what?" she bites out. "For someone who's not worth it? Or maybe it's because I don't exactly look like Celeste?"

I snap my head toward her. "That's bullshit, and you know it."

She whips away from me and tugs on her skirt almost desperately, as if she's trying to cover every inch of exposed skin. Maybe it's her way of erasing what happened between us.

"Leah." I reach for her hand, but she recoils like my fingertips are on fire.

"Don't." Her voice quivers slightly, and it does strange things to my chest. "Not only are you the biggest dick I know, but you're also the biggest coward." A devious little grin tips the side of her mouth. *"You're all I've seen for a long time,"* she taunts, throwing my words back at me. "The Mikhail I thought I knew was a man who always took what he wanted and answered to no one. What are you so afraid of? My dad? Rodrigo?"

"Fear has nothing to do with this. But my family…"

"Save it." Her gaze shifts to my lap. "Maybe you should go take care of that." I follow her line of sight to the stain on my pants. And the memory of her face, contorted with pleasure, hits me with the weight of a freight train.

It takes every morsel of self-restraint not to haul her into my arms. But I know what's at stake. Losing our alliance with the Castellanos would cost millions in product and territory. Fallout is inevitable. I'm the heir to my father's empire, and I can't jeopardize everything we've built…even if that means losing her. The thought is like a thousand serrated knives to the heart. But once this drop is over, I'll keep my distance and let time dull the ache for this woman like it has for four years.

As if sensing the resolution I've come to, Leah shakes her head and pushes to her feet. Benjamin's stupid face flashes in my mind, and I catch her arm before I can stop myself.

"Where are you going?"

"Fuck off."

She attempts to free herself, but I tighten my grasp and tug her back to her seat. Her eyes are wide as she watches me.

"You go to that man, and I'll toss him out of this goddamn plane."

"You're insane."

"Maybe, but I don't make empty threats."

"I'm not afraid of you."

"You?" I feel my expression softening as I touch her cheek, expecting her to lash out, but surprised when she doesn't react or pull away. "You don't ever have to be, pretty girl. But Benny will regret the day he set eyes on you."

My words ignite a flame behind her eyes, and she clenches her fists. I've just given her the perfect opportunity to use her Russian.

"Sir, we're flying into a storm. We have to land."

Looks like Benjamin saved both of our asses.

CHAPTER TEN
LEAH

Road visibility is nearly nonexistent as a snowstorm rages outside. The closest lodging is a group of cabins belonging to a ski resort. The chances of a room being available, let alone two, are slim. Not during this time of year.

My gaze slides to the rearview mirror, and I glimpse Mikhail muttering something into his phone. I hear him address his younger brother, Roman, but he's making it a point to speak low enough so that I can't listen in on their conversation—as if I care. He can go to hell. I'm done with him. Once this drop is over, I'll be on a plane back to Spain, far enough away that I won't ever have to think of him.

Tears ignite beneath my lashes, the lie so bitter that a humorless laugh breaks past my lips.

Who am I kidding?

He meets my eyes in the reflection, but I tear my gaze away, refusing to let him strip any more of my dignity. I'm not sure how we'll make it out of this job without killing each other, but I have never regretted my life choices as much as I do at this very moment.

"I can wait here if you want to check for a vacancy," Conner, our driver, says, addressing me instead of Mikhail, who's seated in the back seat. I'd let him climb in the car first to gauge where he would sit so I could be as far from him as possible. I know it pissed him off. I could feel the fire of his gaze on the back of my head. Thoroughly satisfied, I decided to add more fuel to that blaze and gave him the finger.

"Are you implying that she is the one to step out into this storm?" Mikhail's grave tone causes the man beside me to stiffen. "Surely, you meant that *you* would be right back."

Conner unbuckles his seat belt without a word and is out of the car before my next breath.

"Was that necessary?"

"Absolutely," he deadpans, his attention back on his phone.

"You're insufferable."

"That's not exactly what you were saying today when my fingers were in your pussy."

"Fuck you!"

The wind howls as it pours into the cabin when I throw open the door and make a run for the entrance.

"Leah, get back inside the goddamn car!" Ignoring him, I trudge through the half-foot of snow toward tall glass double doors and hang my face, dodging the icy chill of winter as it bites at my cheeks and sweeps into my lungs.

Fuck, it's freezing.

Mikhail's angry roars reach me as I race past the threshold and into a cozy foyer where dim lights and Christmas decor line a long hallway. I spot our driver standing at the front desk, engaged in what seems to be a heated exchange with the clerk.

"Please, I need a room. You gotta have something, man."

"We're booked. It's five days before Christmas. What you're asking is impossible."

Conner cusses under his breath. Poor guy. He'll sell his soul rather than face Mikhail.

A strong hand suddenly grips my wrist and whirls me around. "You're being childish."

The word triggers something inside me, and I slap him before I can stop myself. With nostrils flaring and a heavy breath rushing from his mouth, he slides a hand into his pocket and, with the other, rubs the reddened spot on his cheek.

"Leah," he grinds out behind clenched teeth. "We need to talk. But not right now, and not like this."

I swallow the knot in my throat. "You're right. Not now or tomorrow." I turn and move toward the two men, both staring us down with wary expressions. "Maybe I'll reach out when I'm back in Barcelona… Or not."

He calls my name again, but I don't turn around.

"Are you okay, miss?" the older man behind the counter asks.

I nod, annoyed that we're arguing in public. "I'm fine."

Before I can say another word, a chorus of alerts blares around us, and in perfect synchronization, we all reach for our cell phones.

Due to the storm, a mandatory county-wide curfew is in effect until 6 a.m. Only then do I notice the wind screeching against the venue's glass, stronger and more turbulent than it was just ten minutes ago.

We're stuck. Not only are we grounded from our flight, but now we're stuck at a resort with no vacancies.

I sigh and rub my temples. All I want is a fucking hot shower and time to myself.

Time away from Mikhail.

"Find a room," I hear him threaten from behind me.

"I— We don't," the clerk stutters. "We don't have a cabin available, sir."

"I'm sure you do. Look again."

A part of me feels awful for the poor clerk having to be subjected to Mikhail's wrath, but I also can't deny that coercing some reserved room where I'll be able to shower and relax is in my best interest. Someone had to have gotten caught up in this storm, unable to make their reservation. Maybe it's selfish, but if anyone can make a deal with the devil himself, it's a Petrov.

"Okay, okay. There's a vacant suite, but if its occupants show up in the morning—"

"Then you'll tell them they've forfeited their room."

The man's mouth opens and closes twice before he decides it's best not to argue with the very large and intimidating Mikhail Petrov.

"It's a honeymoon suite. Includes all the amenities."

Mikhail slides a black card across the counter. "We'll take it."

Honeymoon suite. Does that mean what I'm thinking? There has to be a pull-out sofa. If not, I'm sure he can cozy up in a tub.

The naive, sexually deprived girl from this morning is bouncing at the idea of such a predicament with the man she's been pining for over these last four years. But pissed-the-fuck-off and doubly sexually frustrated Leah from the plane wants to scream.

"Miss, would you like me to grab your bags from the car?"

Conner's gentle question breaks my inner turmoil, and I offer him an appreciative smile and nod, but he doesn't return the gesture. His eyes are fixed behind me, then downcast as he fidgets. Brooding mafia asshole aside, I attribute his lack of confidence to his young age. Conner is handsome and tall, and maybe one day, he'll learn to stand a little straighter.

"Not necessary; I already brought them inside," Mikhail says, placing a hand on the small of my back to lead me away. But I shift my body and twist toward Conner.

"What about you? Where are you staying?"

He shrugs. "Going to wait it out here in the lobby."

"*Leah.*" The way Mikhail says my name will never fail to make my skin tingly, no matter how upset I am, pathetic as it is. "We still have to walk in this mess to get to our cabin. It's best to leave before it gets any worse."

Without acknowledging him, I nod my goodbye to Conner and head down another corridor toward the connecting courtyard where our suite is located. I'm several steps ahead of Mikhail as he has to backtrack and grab our bags before following.

"Why are you trying to provoke me?"

I let out a cynical laugh—the audacity.

"That's an interesting way to spin things."

"You know what I mean. Benny and now that asshole back there."

I come to an abrupt stop and whip around, but it's a move he's not expecting, and he nearly topples me, big hands dropping the metal handles and gripping my waist. He steadies me, but doesn't let go. The urge to melt into his arms is so overwhelming that I have to suck in a breath and look away.

"Who's provoking who? I'm not the one playing games here, Mikki." Shoving him back, I continue down the hall. "You've made your decision clear, and you don't dictate who I can and can't talk to."

"That *kid* couldn't take his eyes off you. He's lucky he's still—"

With a firm finger to his chest, I'm in his face again. "I'm not your property. You don't get to reject me and then get pissed when I breathe in the same vicinity of another man. Who the fuck do you think you are?"

His jaw ticks, pulsing green eyes on mine. "You're Rodrigo's sister, and he asked me to watch out for you."

I scoff and put distance between us, allowing him a few more precious moments of life, because the way I want to beat him with my suitcase is downright unhealthy.

"First, I don't need anyone to watch my back. And you mean the sister whose cum is still on your pants? Wonder what he'd think about that little detail."

Mikhail closes his eyes and grits his teeth. "Enough, Leah."

A grin pulls at my lips when it seems I hit a weakness. "You want to play games, pretend you can resist being with me, but you confessed it yourself." I stalk forward. "I know how I make you feel." My finger trails down his chest. "I know how hard your cock gets for me, Mikhail, just like it did years ago." Pushing to my toes, my lips brush over the stubble on his chin. "The way you made me come for you…"

"Leah…" His hands squeeze my waist.

"How does it feel when I scream your name?" Mikhail's grip grows deliciously painful. "You can't wait to hear it again, can you?"

Our eyes connect, and I know the door to his heart is cracked open, but I don't want to be the one to jump through and get disappointed again. He needs to show me he wants this and is willing to fight for us.

In the meantime, I'll have my fun.

CHAPTER ELEVEN
MIKHAIL

"Curfew lifts in the morning. We should be in the air by ten, at the latest." Dad's quiet for several beats, and I lift the phone from my ear to make sure the call hasn't been disconnected. "You still there?"

Another maddening few seconds crawl by before he clears his throat.

"Everything okay, *Mikhail*?"

When he says my name with a Russian pronunciation, I know that whatever follows is serious, and he'll accept no bullshit. After giving him the rundown on Leah and leaving out what happened between us, his tone shifts, and I can almost hear the wheels in his head turning over different scenarios.

"You know I don't like to miss deadlines or feel like I've lost control."

"Lost control," he repeats, more as a statement than a question.

I relax against the sofa and huff a breath, not in the mood for his cryptic lectures.

"What's your question?"

"You're old enough to make your own decisions. I just hope you know what you're doing here. She's beautiful, but..."

I knew that's where his mind would go.

"Leah is a business partner. Nothing more."

It's not that my father suspects there's ever been anything between us, but he knows the sons he's raised. While loyal to Mom, he brought us up as gods among men. And pussy goes hand in hand with power, respect, and money.

"I don't meddle in your personal life, not even when all that shit happened with Celeste and your divorce, but this girl—you know what's at stake. Emilio might be letting her play the part she wants for now, but he has other plans for her, Mikhail. She's his prized possession."

The thought of Leah being seen as a pawn and nothing more than a means to gain wealth sets my blood on fire. I can offer her everything, give her the whole goddamn world, but it's not good enough.

Pure bloodlines, I heard her father say once. It's bullshit.

"How's your wife? And the baby?" I ask, choosing to change the subject.

He releases a quiet sigh, as if deciding not to press any further. "They're good."

I don't miss how his tone brightens. A part of me is happy that he's found someone after all these years. But I won't lie. The thought of him fucking his now-dead best friend's daughter, then subsequently marrying her, is still a hard pill to swallow. She's years younger than Roman and Lev–younger than Leah–and pregnant with my little sister.

Now-dead best friend.

I turn those words over in my thoughts and laugh at the irony and similarities of our situation.

My attention focuses on the black door across the room, where the sound of running water suddenly stops.

I don't have to wonder if I'd do the same for Leah, because I know the answer. I've killed for her in the past. And if it comes down to Rodrigo and Emilio…

"Son, are you still there?"

My father pulls me from the vision of both men dead by my hand. "Yeah," I say, my eyes drifting back to the shadow of Leah's feet beneath the door. "I'll send you a text once we've landed tomorrow."

I offer a quick goodbye and toss my cell onto a side table as I close my eyes and indulge in her voice filtering across the room. She's singing loud enough for me to hear and know it's Spanish, but low enough that I can't make out the lyrics even if I understood them.

Leah walking back into my life as my partner, what we did on that plane, and how we ended up in this room together makes my mind reel. She can't imagine the guilt and torture I've lived with for the past four years.

Fisting the edge of the couch, I nearly spring to my feet and barrel through the goddamn door. But I cover my face with my hands as I drop my head against the cushion and exhale a flustered breath.

Leah will be my end; I just know it.

No sooner does the thought manifest, she opens the door, wrapped in nothing but a short white towel, and strolls across the room toward the bed. Her long, dark hair is in a messy bun. And my cock's reaction is instant.

It's the effect she's going for. Purposely fucking with me. While she looks like she's idly going about a routine, there's tension in her movements. They're calculated.

Leaning my elbows on my knees, I give her exactly what she wants and drink her in, from her perfectly manicured toes and tanned legs to the edges of every delicious curve where parts of her shoulders are still dotted with water droplets. My dick pushes painfully against the seam of my zipper as I imagine how soft and warm her skin must feel, fresh from a shower.

The urge to taste her, to run my tongue over every inch of her body, forces me to my feet before I realize I'm even moving.

"I hope you like to sleep on the floor, Mikki," she says, tone brimming with malice as she loosens the towel and lets it drift to the floor. Without a second glance in my direction, she climbs into the bed and slips under the sheets.

Goddamn her.

"You mind flipping the lights. I'm exhausted."

Within a breath, I'm at the bedside and catch the stiffness in her shoulders when she feels my presence at her back, sliding in behind her.

"You're playing games, pretty girl, as if you don't understand the bigger picture."

She shivers when my words reach her, mouth brushing over her ear.

"You say you're not interested, so the fact that I'm naked under here isn't your concern."

Slipping a hand beneath the comforter, I find the curve of her hip and dig my fingers into her skin. A low whimper falls from her lips when I haul her toward me.

"Why are you naked, *krasivaya devushka?*" I ask, like the masochist fuck I am.

"You know why," she whispers, then pushes her ass into my erection. "We're alone...miles away from reality." Leah guides my hand to her breast and squeezes, coaxing me to do the same—not that I need motivation. "Touch me."

There's no turning back once I have her again.

"Leah..." I rasp, pressing her closer until the contact is nearly painful, both physically and emotionally. I'm punishing myself as a reminder that she isn't mine to keep, just as she wasn't four years ago.

"Don't call me Leah. I know I mean more to you than that."

"Of course you do."

She relaxes, letting her body mold against mine, and I kiss on her shoulder.

"Do I?"

"I can't have you…because I'll never let go."

"You're a coward, Mikhail," she says with a slight shake in her voice as she flips to face me. Tears distort her beautiful brown eyes.

I use my thumb to gently tug at her bottom lip where it's tucked tightly between her teeth, as if choking back a sob. "Pretty girl, don't cry."

"I'm so stupid. I thought maybe after four years, things would be different. But you're a disgrace to your name."

Her words cut deeper than any physical pain I've ever endured.

CHAPTER TWELVE
LEAH

The lobby is fairly quiet this early in the morning, especially after last night's storm. From the corner of my eye, I see Mikhail's hulking figure pacing furiously just outside the front entrance. Equipped with sound and weatherproof glass, I can only catch a whisper of his rage as he roars obscenities into the phone, evident by the veins protruding from his neck, even at a distance. Whoever is on the other end of that call is getting their ass handed to them. I want to care. I should, since I know he's talking to his flight staff, and whatever news they're giving him doesn't seem good.

But sadly, I don't.

I'm far too exhausted from the emotional whiplash that is Mikhail Petrov. The more time I spend with him, the more I want to fuck him, hold him—and stab him in the carotid.

Sighing, I shift my gaze away toward a brick fireplace. I'm close enough to feel the heat warm my cheeks, and it's exactly what I need at that moment as I close my eyes and tune out the distant voice of the man driving me to the edges of my sanity.

Last night, he'd slept on a love seat, and a part of me, the one

stupidly in love, couldn't help feeling slightly guilty as his 6'4"
massive frame dwarfed the large piece of furniture. I woke up to him
contorted in a way that should have left him with the mother of all
cricks in his neck.

Despite the disaster that occurred between us, I threw a fleece
blanket over his body before heading to the bathroom.

"Glad to see you survived the storm."

Conner's unexpected voice catches me off guard. His tone is
bright, though the bags painted beneath his eyes let me know his night
wasn't all that restful.

"I did. Did you end up crashing in the lobby after all?"

He sticks his hands in his pockets and sways as he nods. "Wasn't
so bad. They were nice enough to give me a blanket."

"I'm glad," I say, flashing him a friendly smile. "Are you heading
out?"

"Got word the roads should be cleared in about an hour."

His fidgeting becomes more apparent. He's nervous, mouth
thinning as if he's debating a question he's unsure he should ask.
Surely, he isn't thinking of asking for my number. While Mikhail and I
don't behave like a couple, it's pretty bold of him to assume otherwise.
But I remain quiet and patient so he can get on with it. Maybe this is
why I've always preferred older men—*and when I say older, I mean
only Mikhail*—because guys my age are so immature and indecisive.
Or maybe I'm just hopelessly biased since indecision seems to be a
trend in my life, regardless of the source.

Conner scratches the back of his head and draws a breath. "That
guy you're here with…are you two—"

"Why don't you fucking stutter some more? Maybe she'll
understand you better."

Mikhail's harsh words startle Conner, who cringes and whirls
back to where my partner stands against the door, leveling him with a

murderous glare.

Rolling my eyes, I push to my feet and stand between them. "Don't take your bad mood out on others, Mikki. Conner here was just about to invite me to breakfast."

Maybe using this poor kid to fuck with Mikhail is low, especially as his eyes widen and ping between us in a panic. But I'm feeling particularly petty.

"Was he now?"

"Uh, no…I-I was just saying goodbye."

Conner isn't a small guy. He's just a few inches shorter than the man plotting his death. But darkness lives in the eyes of the Petrov men and the way they carry themselves like predators among prey. Demanding respect and reverence while dominating every room they step foot in. I know that look all too well. It's the same one I've been surrounded by my whole life.

Made men.

And like in every species, the strong sniff out the weak and vice versa.

"I have to get back to work. Hope you all make it to where you're headed." Conner spares me a half smile and retreats down a back hallway.

"Has anyone ever told you your people skills suck?"

Mikhail shrugs. "I don't need people skills."

Cocky bastard.

"So?" I ask as he moves with purpose toward the front desk. "When do we leave?"

"We don't," he deadpans.

I trail behind him. "What does that mean?"

Mikhail runs a hand through his hair, the stress evident in the harsh exhale fleeing his lungs. Yet his gaze unexpectedly softens when it finds mine.

"The storm must have fucked the plane. Something about lines freezing over. It's undergoing maintenance and probably won't be ready for another day."

"Shit. The drop is this evening."

"Yeah. Shit."

"Can't you just rent another one? Do you need me to contact Rod?"

He drags in another breath of air, as if calling on every ounce of patience in his body. It strikes me then that Mikhail has never had to answer to anyone. Feelings of insecurity suddenly creep in as I wonder if he finds my line of questioning and company annoying.

"Don't worry about all that," he says, his tone surprisingly tender. "I've made some phone calls, and we'll be good until tomorrow."

"So what now?"

A thrill runs through me at the thought of another night alone in a room with this man—and then I want to slap myself.

"I have to ensure we're good in the suite for one more night. Why don't you get us a table for breakfast, and I'll meet you in a few."

I say nothing as I head for the lobby until he catches my wrist and tugs me back to his side. The steel behind his eyes is gone, replaced by the sparkle of a smile.

"Hey, are we good?"

"Why wouldn't we be, Mikki?" I tease, clapping his chest.

I'm willing to bet money, my idea of *good* dramatically differs from his.

As I motion to leave, he stops me again. "Leah, I've done a lot of thinking. And things between us are not what I want them to be in so many ways. But I'm asking—no, begging—for us to put it all aside for now. And I know I don't have any right to ask that of you. But the last thing I want is to argue and see you upset."

The sincerity in his eyes slash at every weak point in my resolve, but unsure how to respond, I simply continue toward the lobby without looking back.

Deciding to play it cool while we eat, I pretend our confessions and everything that happened between us in the last twenty-four hours was just a fever dream, because as I listen to him speak, I remember how much I enjoy his company without pressure and expectations. It's the first time I feel completely at ease since our reunion, bringing me to the conclusion that maybe his proposal of a temporary truce is for the best.

A soothing sense of warmth spreads through my chest as I watch his hard exterior melt away while he relays his plans for Christmas and the anticipation of seeing his family after months.

Of course, I ignore my inner whore pointing out the fact that I'm also shamelessly wet.

Sue me.

"Your dad is having a baby?" I ask with genuine shock, and he nods.

Mr. Nikolai is a very handsome man and the epitome of a silver fox. No wonder his sons are blessed with good looks and egos to match. I've met most of them over the years to some capacity.

"Congrats. Whew! That poor girl. I already feel for her." I chuckle, shaking my head.

He grins but agrees. "I haven't met her yet, but family is family. And Natalia, the baby, my brother's wife—all have their place in mine."

Twinges of envy ripple through me at the realization that Mikhail doesn't consider me part of his circle. Averting my eyes, I swallow back the lump in my throat. But not before he catches the disappointment on my face.

Reaching for my hand, he rasps, "*Moya krasivaya devochka, ty samaya vazhnaya.*" (My beautiful girl, you're the most important one.)

But I slip from his grip and refuse to meet his eyes. I won't allow him to reel me in again.

"Don't say that if you don't mean it."

"I may be a lot of things, pretty girl, but a liar isn't one of them."

I beg to differ.

The small cafe isn't the place to rehash the past, so soon after we agreed to keep things light. Instead of responding or diving across this table and strangling him, I scan the room, searching for a change in subject. A framed white sign advertising skiing and snowmobile rides catches my eye.

Having never skied in my life, I opt not to die on these slopes. And on the other hand, how hard could driving a snowmobile be? It looks similar to a jet ski, and I've been on plenty of those.

"Mikhail, let's do something fun."

His eyebrows draw together. "Something...*fun?*"

"Yeah, you know that thing normal people do when they're not working 24/7? If we're stuck here, we might as well make the most of it."

I can think of at least five positions that would also work in this scenario...

MIKHAIL PETROV   93

CHAPTER THIRTEEN
MIKHAIL

"Leah! Goddamnit!"

Snow sprays into the front of my visor, momentarily blocking my view as I trail behind her. She's gunning through the marked path, barely dodging trees and small boulders, forcing me to push my vehicle to the limits to catch up.

I don't know what made me agree to do this, but I felt I couldn't say no after everything I've put her through. Leah was so excited that she didn't finish her meal before dragging me to a clothing and supply store off the main lobby. But what should have been a quick trip to pick up necessities and proper attire ended up being an hours-long ordeal.

"Slow down!" I yell, swerving away from the top of a half-buried shrub.

I know she can't hear me—or hell, maybe she can and is choosing to be reckless. A fleeting vision of her over my knee, wearing nothing but my handprints on her ass for being a brat, jolts straight to my cock.

Fuck.

Before I can spiral down that rabbit hole, I see her veer off an unmarked path, and I wonder if she realizes her mistake or knowingly decides to take the scenic route.

I follow her through the winding woods and attempt to flag her down.

"Leah, pullover!"

She twists in my direction as I flail my arm like a goddamn maniac and lifts a gloved hand, waving in response before accelerating and raining down another monsoon of snow onto my face and lap.

"Fuck. Just wait until I catch you."

Another twenty minutes tick by as we drive deeper into the darkening path. I'd be lying if I said I'm not enjoying myself.

Fun, huh?

It's been a long time since I've experienced this level of exhilaration. As someone who thrives on predictability and structure, I'm surprised that the fact we have no fucking clue where we're heading almost makes the moment more thrilling. Reminiscent of the euphoria I used to feel in her arms.

Leah's snowmobile slows, and I follow until we both come to a stop. I stay seated and fold my arms over my chest as she climbs off hers and removes her helmet.

When I catch sight of her beaming smile, all traces of aggravation disappear.

She's so fucking beautiful it hurts.

"I'm glad you could keep up," she teases, shaking out her long hair.

I say nothing as she straddles my vehicle and faces me, leaning her elbows back on the console. Her snowsuit is thick with warm layers but fitted enough that I'm mesmerized by the silhouette of her soft curves. What I would give to take her right here.

She's yours. Take what's yours.

"You're crazy, pretty girl. We're out here in the middle of

nowhere." Sliding off my helmet, I look around at the miles of endless forest. "What if we get caught in another storm?"

"Doesn't sound so bad," she murmurs, tipping her head back and blowing steam into the cold air. "I like this. That crisp chill smells and tastes so good. Such a difference from Dallas, don't you think?"

"Does it remind you of your time in New York?" I question, letting the steam billow out of my mouth as well.

"It's different." She leans, hands braced against the seat between us. "The city is beautiful, of course, but this— Something about this is almost…otherworldly."

Her gaze tips to the darkening sky, and her dreamy voice sounds as if she wants me to follow and confirm. But I can't will myself to look away when all the beauty and awe she's describing is already in front of me.

As if feeling the heat of my stare, Leah's eyes fall back to mine, and she smiles as I inch closer, drawn to her lips like a magnet.

"Your nose is cold and a little red," I say, kissing the tip.

"My mouth is cold, too." Her whisper is barely audible, but I feel the vulnerable plea as it rushes through me, pushing me to close the small distance even though I know I shouldn't.

Despite the chill in the air, her lips are plush, and they taste sweet, like some type of berry. I want more. So much more.

Gripping her hips, I pull her into my lap, exactly where I need her, as she grinds her sweet little cunt against me in a tortuous rocking motion.

"This is how it's supposed to be, Mikhail."

With a fist in her hair, I tug her head, exposing her neck and nicking my teeth along the skin until I find her pulse point and use my tongue to savor the way her body reacts to me. She truly has no clue how hard it is to resist being close to her and not tearing off every *fucking* piece of clothing.

Shoving her back against the console, I reach for the zipper on her suit, giving in for just a moment.

Just one goddamn taste.

She watches me with intent. Her soft breaths spur me on as I shove her shirt above the black lace bra encasing her gorgeous tits. And I wonder if she knew this would be how this little trip would go down.

"I don't think I've ever stopped thinking about the way you taste and feel," I say, kissing and biting the thin fabric. "It's a high I've been chasing for years."

Leah holds each side of my head firmly, forcing me to look at her. "I don't want to picture you trying to forget me in the arms of other women."

She's right. That's exactly what I've done for the last four fucking years. But I was fooling myself.

"I won't lie to you." I kiss down her trembling abs. "But it's always been you, pretty girl. Always in my *fucking* head," I growl into the skin below her navel, then chuckle at the memory of a date from hell when I'd said Leah's name instead of the woman bent over my desk. When that bitch clocked me with her heel on the back of the head, I may have contemplated tossing her out the eighth-story window of my office.

"Mikhail," she breathes out, fingers tightly wound in my hair as I press a kiss between her thighs. Still wearing her snow pants, she arches into me and begs, "More…more, please."

I dip my hand into her panties, and my mouth waters as my fingers slide over her clit, coating every inch with her arousal. "Oh, fuck."

When I pull away, she whines in protest until I use my slick fingers to paint up her stomach and in between her breasts. Our eyes connect as I move over her collarbone, then drag them to her chin as she licks her lips in anticipation.

"You're my drug and my poison wrapped into one beautifully diabolical package," I say as I trace the contours of her mouth before pushing inside, where her eager tongue laps at every drop. "Like savoring heaven with the promise of hell."

Tears trickle from the corners of her eyes, and I press my lips to the droplets.

"Fuck, *krasivaya devushka*. Just know you're going to spend a lot of time naked and wet. Exactly how you were made to be for me." When I push my fingers deeper down her throat, she gags, the sound making my cock throb.

A swift vibration startles me. My phone buzzes in my pocket, but I ignore the damn thing, not willing to tear myself from her.

We must be closer to civilization than we thought, considering there's a signal out here in what seems like the middle of nowhere.

When the vibration goes off again, I curse under my breath and reach into my coat.

"Mikhail, there's a Sig strapped to my thigh. Don't make me use it on you. If you pick up that call..." Leah's fists bunch up my collar.

"Wasn't planning on it, but I'm debating if smashing it against a tree is worth it."

She laughs and pulls me to her lips as I peek at the screen. And just like that, reality comes knocking again. The name Emilio Castellanos lights up the device. It's a rare occasion when he calls. In the decade since our alliance, he's only contacted me personally a handful of times, if that. All our dealings are handled through Rodrigo and vice versa.

A cold chill races up my body. Not out of fear, but the threat he'd made all those years ago echoes in my mind. I may be friends with Rod, but Emilio isn't loyal to anyone but himself and his blood. And he all but threatened death on my brothers and me if he ever got a whiff that I wanted anything with his daughter.

Our partnership has always been wrought with tension, but he knows he benefits just as much as we do.

Leah notes my hesitation and looks at the screen.

"Forget him," she says, shaking her head. "This is about us. None of them matter."

"You're right. I don't give a single fuck about what he thinks about me. But—"

"Mikhail…" There's a tremor in her voice. "You better choose your next words wisely."

I frame her face and sigh. "Pretty girl—"

"Oh, fuck you!" Shoving me back, she bolts toward her snowmobile and turns the engine.

"Leah, wait," I call, but she takes off before I can get another word in. "Goddamnit."

CHAPTER FOURTEEN
LEAH

Red lights in the distance draw my attention as I break the forest line and reach the end of an embankment. I don't give myself time to sit and sulk because the tears searing the backs of my eyes are threatening to spill over, and I'm done crying.

The moon is high in the sky, illuminating the thin layer of fresh snow on a concrete walkway leading toward what looks to be a small tavern.

Exactly what I need. A *fucking* drink, or ten.

I make the short trek across the way, but pause and glance at the tree line, half-expecting to see Mikhail emerging in a rage. But it's eerily quiet, and I hate that a part of me is worried if he's lost or cold… or…

Stop it.

Pushing that man out of my thoughts, I tug at the heavy metal door and step through the threshold. A little bell signaling my arrival chimes above my head. In an instant, the entire establishment goes silent. All heads turn in my direction, a flurry of whispers reaching my ears.

Fuck. Where in the wrong turn am I?

Taking in the faces of the patrons, all men, it's obvious they're not used to seeing someone like me, especially stumbling in on such a cold night.

I sigh and decide right then I have exactly zero fucks left to give. And this girl needs a drink. But it doesn't take long for disappointment to rear its ugly head when I realize I don't have my wallet.

Seconds tick by, and I know I have to make a decision or risk looking like a fucking loose cannon just standing here, doing and saying nothing. A low whistle echoes from somewhere to my left, and it dawns on me then—when have I ever paid for my own drink?

"It's warm in here," I say in my most sultry voice as I fan myself for extra theatrics. It's not a lie. Hot air blazes from a vent on the ceiling directly above me.

The need for a moment of relief from life is greater than my pride, so I slide my zipper down to my hips and pull my arms free from the sleeves. Another wave of complete silence falls over the tavern, and the heat of every single pair of eyes sears into me.

Zero fucks.

I pull out a stool at the bar, and the bartender approaches with a sly smile.

"Ma'am, can I start you anything."

"A water," I say, pretending to look over a menu. He nods and pours me a glass.

"You lost or something, sweetheart?" a man with short blond hair and a clean shave asks as he slides onto the stool beside mine.

Here we go.

"Well, seeing as I'm exactly where I intended to be, the answer is no, I'm not."

He chuckles and rubs his hairless chin.

"Well, I like that answer. Can I buy you a drink?" Leaning in a little too closely, he places a hand on the back of my chair and glances at my glass of water before returning his gaze to my tits. "Do you drink, Miss…?"

"Lena," I reply, trying not to roll my eyes. "Yes, I do."

Just one drink.

"How about I have Anderson here make you one of his specials." I raise an eyebrow, alarms going off as I catch the bartender wink in what he thinks is a subtle gesture.

My need to drink does not supersede my safety. While I'm armed, there are far too many of them. And looking a little more closely, the walls are adorned with strange plaques and emblems, along with photographs of what look to be the same men sitting around me. Maybe this isn't a bar, after all, but some kind of club.

"You know, I didn't catch your name, but actually, I'm heading out. Maybe next time." As I motion to stand, he grabs my arm.

"Come on, *Lena,*" he taunts, saying my name with an accent. "Sit." His command is exactly what I need to tip over the edge of a blind rage.

"You need to let go. I won't ask twice."

"*Oh!*" His stupid mouth opens into an exaggerated O as he tightens his hold on me. "Tell me, sweetheart? What will you do? Scream?"

"No, that's your job."

There's a twitch in his eye for the briefest of seconds as understanding seems to dawn, but it comes half a second too late. My hand is around the hilt of a steak knife, and before he can react, I stab it into the hand he has resting on the wooden counter.

His pained howl pierces the establishment, drawing everyone's attention.

"Goddamn you! Get that bitch."

Chairs screech against the hardwood as the men break to their feet in their attempts to reach me before I can get to the door, but I yank it open in time and sprint around back toward the snowy path. I'm banking on them not knowing which direction I came from.

The slick sheet of snow has very little traction, and I find myself slipping and stumbling like a fucking baby deer. But the snowmobile is just a few feet away, and I'll be home free.

You're so stupid.

I should have walked out of there the moment my instincts screamed for me to do so, but I let this shit with Mikhail get the best of me.

Damn him and damn them.

As I reach the embankment, a wave of relief washes over me, but the moment is short-lived. I hit the ground with so much force that it pushes the air out of my lungs, causing pain to explode in my chest.

My mouth parts, but nothing comes out, just shallow, agonized groans.

Shit.

I was totally kidding about the whole 'wrong turn' thing, yet here I am, starring in my own twisted version.

Mustering the strength to get on my hands and knees, I make a move for my gun. But whoever this bastard is yanks my hair and tosses me on my back.

The bartender, Anderson, is standing over me, holding a shotgun with a sadistic grin on his face. I've killed a man before, and as much as he deserved it, it wasn't something I enjoyed. But the way this stranger is looking at me like I'm an object made for his depraved satisfaction lets me know he's done this before.

"It's rude to leave without a goodbye. You didn't even tip."

"Fuck you." I make another attempt to reach for my side piece, but he sees my intention and raises the shotgun.

"I'll blow a hole through that pretty face of yours if you don't relax," he warns, steadying his aim. "All we wanted was to have a little fun. You wouldn't have remembered a goddamn thing, and we all would have gone about our lives as if none of this had ever happened." He kicks my legs open. "But you think you're some bad bitch, don't you, sweetheart?"

The front end of his boot pushes against my center, and I clamp down on my jaw, willing back my anger because pissing him off won't help. I have to be smart about this.

"You'll never see me again. I promise. I don't even live here," I plead, putting on my best damsel act.

"I let you go, and the feds will be knocking on my door by morning. You fucked this up, not me. And poor Simmons is in there, bleeding out all over my fucking bar. You owe me, and I intend to collect." Leaning the barrel of the gun on the ground, he flashes another one of his psychotic smiles and motions with his chin. "Take off your top."

I stare him down in defiance. If I'm going to die, I'll go out fighting.

"I'm not going to do that."

"Bitch, you have two seconds before I—"

It takes several beats to register what my eyes are seeing. Blood gushes from the man's throat, where the jagged edge of a thick branch is protruding like something out of a horror movie. Red splashes onto my legs, staining my suit.

"Are you hurt?" Mikhail's voice is strained, eyes wild, as he scans me from head to toe.

"No."

The bartender is still twitching and attached to the branch when Mikhail tosses him to the side and lunges for me.

"Look at me. Did he touch you? Did he hurt you?"

"No, but we have to get out of here. There's more of them."

"Chasing you?"

"Yeah," I say as he tugs me to my feet and cradles my chin. "You think I'm going to let that slide? No one threatens what's mine."

He snatches the shotgun from Anderson, who's finally dead, and turns his back to me, headed toward the tavern. "Leah, get back to the resort."

"Fuck that! You either come with me or we do this together. It's your choice, because I'm not leaving."

He drags in a flustered breath. I know the instinct to protect those he cares for is pulling him to those men. But eight against two are not good odds. And I'm banking on the fact that he cares more about my well-being than getting revenge—at least for now.

"Mikhail?"

With a strong swing of his arm, the shotgun whirls into the air and sinks into a mound of snow. Before I can question him, he grabs my hand, and we make a run toward my snowmobile.

"Hold on tight," he says as the vehicle roars to life, and we plunge into the dark forest.

MIKHAIL PETROV 109

CHAPTER FIFTEEN
LEAH

I'm not sure how close we are to the cabins or how far from that hell hole back there, but I need a moment. My head is spinning with so many what-ifs.

"Stop. Stop, please, stop," I beg, frantically tapping on his thigh.

The snowmobile decelerates, and I don't even wait for it to come to a complete stop before I climb off and find a tree to lean on. Nausea churns my stomach, and I hang my head, hoping to vomit. That's when I see the splatters of blood staining my pants and boots, and I want to crawl out of my skin. I know it's freezing. My exposed arms are cold to the touch, but I'm too high on adrenaline to feel a damn thing.

"I have to get this off!"

As I shove the snowsuit down my hips, Mikhail touches my arm, and I freeze.

"Hey, let me help you."

Silence passes between us before either one moves or says anything.

"Okay," I finally reply, and he wastes no time dropping to his knees to undo my boots.

Another stretch of silence, and I know what he's doing. He's gathering his thoughts, trying to string together the right words so that he doesn't come off like an asshole. But I know he's upset. What I did wasn't smart.

I step on the suit and use it as a barrier against the snow as Mikhail strips off his coat and drapes it over my shoulders, surprising me when he grabs one of my arms and shoves it into the massive sleeve, then the other. Our eyes connect, and the moment he takes a breath and rakes his hands against the sides of his head, I know he's ready to unleash hell.

"Why did you run off like that? That man could have… What if I hadn't gotten there when I did?"

"I know, I know. It was stupid, but how was I supposed to know I walked into a wolf's den? I just wanted a drink."

His eyes widen, and he shakes his head with indignation. "A goddamn drink?"

"I don't need this right now."

Mikhail grabs my shoulders, hands shaking. "Do you know what that would have done to me? If something would have happened to you."

The fucking audacity.

"You don't get to do this."

"The hell I don't!"

I shove him back and sacrifice my socks to snow as I trudge past him. "After tomorrow, we go our separate ways, and I go back to living my life, Mikhail. I go to bars at night. I take walks. I fucking *live*, okay? Without you." I throw his coat at him and immediately regret it as the cold sears through my skin, down to the bones. But I can't let him know that. "You don't get to worry about me because you've made it painfully clear that I'm not at the top of your list of priorities." My voice cracks. "That I'm not worth fighting for."

I turn and walk away, and it's dumb because where the hell am I even going?

"Leah." His voice is surprisingly soft. "You ran off because you refused to listen to what I had to say."

"I've heard your script enough." Maybe the cabins aren't too far from here. I can just walk the rest of the way.

Are you stupid?

Yes.

But I keep moving anyway.

"Leah, stop."

"Why?" My whisper is barely audible, and I don't realize I'm crying until a salty tear rolls into the corner of my mouth.

"Because I've been stupid too."

I hear his words, but there's no time to process them because, in the next second, he whirls me around and hoists me onto his waist.

"I'm so fucking sorry, *moya lyubov'* (my love). No one else matters to me but you. I promise you that." He uses his thumb to wipe my tears. "If having you means starting a war, I'll watch the world burn in your arms...then build you a new one."

He leans in and grazes my lips as a low groan rattles in his chest. "I love you, pretty girl. I've loved you for a fucking long time."

For once, I'm speechless. The words I've been waiting to hear for so long have short-circuited my brain. Looping my arms behind his neck, I rest my forehead against his and close my eyes. I'm trembling, and I don't know if it's the cold or my body's reaction to his confession.

"I'll never forgive myself," he whispers, kissing up my jaw. "But I need you to say something."

"It's about damn time."

We erupt into laughter, and he squeezes me tighter. "I plan to make it up to you every single day," he promises, then sets me down on the snowmobile and wraps me in his coat. "Let's get back."

But I shake my head and let it slide off my shoulders. "No, you've made me wait long enough, Mikhail Petrov." I place my arms behind me and lean on the seat, letting my thighs fall open. "I need you to fuck me right here, right now."

"Leah, it's too goddamn cold." He chuckles, stepping between my thighs. "And I want to be able to see you fully when I make love to you."

I reach for the waistband of his pants and run my hand over his erection. "You worried about the cold, Mikki?" I tease with a wink. "And I never said I wanted you to make love to me." Sliding his zipper down, I reach in and stroke his hard length, eager to be utterly broken by this man and put back together.

Over and over.

His hands tangle in my hair as he dips down to kiss me.

"As much as I want to have you right now, you're half-naked, it's freezing, and my balls are shriveling up into my body as we speak."

I can't help the laughter that bubbles up my throat, but when his expression turns serious, I quiet down, and we find each other's eyes in the darkness.

"I also want to be sure you're okay," he says, bringing the coat back over my shoulders.

I rise to my knees and pull him in for another kiss. This is the Mikhail so very few know, and I have the privilege of being the woman he lets his guard down with.

CHAPTER SIXTEEN
MIKHAIL

"Get back here."

I pluck her from the doorway and lift her bridal style before stepping through the entrance of our cabin. The sound of her laughter warms my chest. I'll never tire of it. It's one of the first things I grew to love about her. She was and will always be the brightest light in my life. Nearly losing her tonight was a moment of reckoning.

On the drive back, I tormented myself with all the scenarios that could have played out had I not gotten to her in time. Every single one ended with me in prison or dead because living without her is not an option.

Not anymore. Not ever.

Kicking the bathroom door open, I place her on the vanity, tossing aside the damn coat. Next is her shirt, followed quickly by the black bra.

"*Ya tebya lyublyu,*" (I love you.) I say, covering her nipple with my mouth.

Nails against my scalp, she tips her head back and releases the sweetest little moan. I've never forgotten the way she sang for me. It's stayed imprinted in my memories through the years as torment.

"I love you, too," she whispers, winding her legs around my torso and pulling me in as I kiss down her body, teeth and tongue savoring every inch.

"What did you say out there earlier? You want me to do what?" My questions go unanswered, replaced by a gasp when I bite down on her tight nipple.

"Shit…" she whines as my teeth mark the other.

"Say it," I growl, hand around her throat.

Leah locks eyes with me and grins. "I want you to fuck me hard and fast. Make me cry…then do it again."

As much as I want to take my time worshiping her the way she deserves, tearing her apart is precisely what we both need. I've gone too fucking long without this woman.

My clothes fall to the floor next to hers.

"I don't think there's anything you could ask for that I won't give you," I say, her hair clutched in my hand. "That's the power you have over me, pretty girl. Only you."

"So shut up and fuck me already." She chuckles over my lips and strokes my cock firm and slow, forcing me to double over and bite down on her shoulder.

"I need you to know that you're mine." I lift one of her legs and then the other, her feet on the vanity, as I indulge my eyes in her beautiful cunt, open and dripping for me. "You're going to be my wife." Pressing my thumb to her clit, I rub tight circles. "Have my babies."

"Fuck…Mikhail." She gasps when I push two fingers inside, finding that spot that makes her tremble.

"You're going to be my queen, Leah."

I lick up her wet slit, and her thighs shake around my head as I devour her like the sweetest goddamn fruit.

"I'm taking you home with me. Not another day without you, my love."

She bucks her hips with every stroke, sharp nails piercing my scalp. I could die between her legs, but I need to claim what's mine. Throwing her knee over my shoulder and pressing one last kiss to her swollen pussy, I straighten and align myself at her entrance.

"Do it," she begs, rocking forward.

"My pretty girl, begging me to fuck her." As I slide inside, she hisses, body stiffening slightly as I spread her open. "God, I missed you."

Smoothing my hands under her ass, I angle her toward me. "Just like that," I rasp, bottoming out inside her and stilling for a moment as I regain my composure. She's so goddamn tight that it feels like her pussy is choking my dick. "This sweet cunt was made for me."

Home.

Everything falls into place.

The chase is over.

I slam into her at a steady rhythm, and she meets me thrust for thrust.

"Mikhail… God, I love you."

I make a mental note to keep my hair long for her, relishing the delicious sting of her fingers as she clutches harder the closer she rises to her release. Our mouths collide in desperate need, teeth clashing as we fight to consume the other first.

More.

Pulling out, I grip her hips and allow her a whine at the loss of contact because it's fucking music to my black soul.

"I'll kill you," she threatens, voice ragged.

I chuckle and kiss her, swallowing her protests before flipping her over on her hands and knees. Stroking my slick cock, I dip to bite an ass cheek, then the other, and she whimpers my name.

"Hands on the mirror and spread your knees for me. I want you to see how pretty you look when I tongue-fuck you."

I planned to sink back inside her, but seeing my girl on her knees, beautiful round ass in my face, I can't resist.

Leah does as she's told, and with one hand on my cock, I lean in and flick her swollen clit, lapping and sucking at her arousal until her body quivers and she breaks apart, crying out my name.

"Oh, fuck," I groan when a flush of wetness drips down her legs onto the counter, in the sink, and even the floor. "Goddamn, baby. Did you just—squirt?"

I find her hooded eyes in the mirror as her chest rises and falls in quick pants, leaving her unable to speak. She rests her forehead against the glass and gives me a lazy nod.

"I… I've never…done that," she manages to say, leaning back on her calves and sighing.

"That was the sexiest thing I've ever seen."

I loop my arm around her waist and pull her off the vanity, bending her over and sinking inside as far as she can take me.

Every thrust sends her gliding across her own mess, and it's fucking glorious. I wrap my fist in her hair and tug her head back, pitching my voice close to her ear. "Look at you, my love. Look what we did," I say, eyes on her glistening tits as they bounce and droplets trickle off her skin.

"Harder, Mikki, fuck me harder. You owe me."

I shove her forward, pressing her chest against the marble, feet off the floor, and pound into her with delicious cruelty.

"You said"—thrust—"to make you"—thrust—"cry" I snake a hand around her hip and find her swollen clit—"and I already did."

"Fuck, yes."

Leah tightens around my cock, her mouth parting against the hard surface as she shudders and screams. I'm right there with her, falling over the edge and driving into her until every drop is spent.

"Mikhail...*yes*. I love you," she confesses breathlessly.

I kiss her shoulder blade. "I love you."

"I'm starving."

With a laugh, I straighten and slide out of her. "Let's feed you. You're going to need the energy."

As Leah maneuvers herself off the vanity, I grab an ass cheek in each hand and open her up, reveling in how my cum is slipping out of her. I slide two fingers over the dripping seam and circle her sensitive clit, making her jerk.

It suddenly hits me that we didn't discuss nor use protection—slight panic flares.

"My love, are you on..."

She nods, as if reading my thoughts. "I am."

Leah *will* bear my children one day. But for now, I need her to myself.

"Are you falling asleep on me?" Leah squeezes my thigh, and I tighten my hold on her waist beneath the water.

"No," I lie, the thickness of my voice betraying me.

She smiles and arches her chin, kissing my jaw. "Liar."

"Fine. You caught me."

"We can head back inside if you're tired. I might even consider sharing the bed tonight."

Her body shakes with my laughter. "Is that right? After all the orgasms I've given you, that's how you'd repay me? By making me sleep on that goddamn couch again."

Leah pokes a toe out of the water as she pretends to mull over the decision. I let her have her fun. My mind is elsewhere. I gaze beyond the deck and the steam that rises and swirls above the hot tub's surface as it clashes with the frigid night air. The forest is pitch black in the distance, but somewhere out there, beyond the line of trees, is a group of men who deserve to die.

While Leah was in the bathroom, I searched their exact location, the names of their members, addresses, rap sheets—the whole fucking nine—and called in a few favors. I'll deal with them myself, but slipping away from her is impossible. I know she's capable, but I'll never willingly put my girl in harm's way.

"Where'd you go?" she asks, caressing my face.

I take her hand and press a kiss on her palm. "I'm right here."

There's a beat of silence, and she tenses. I can sense a question hanging in the air.

"Ask," I urge, giving her a reassuring squeeze.

Leah pulls my hand to her lips to return the gesture and sighs. "Celeste. Can I ask what happened?"

"You can ask me anything. I have nothing to hide from you."

She twists in my lap, now straddling me, her vulnerable gaze on mine. "You were married almost three years. Did you ever love her?"

"No. I'll admit I tried. But you can't force that shit. Learned the hard way." I place my hands on her neck and caress her cheeks with my thumbs. "But it was the only way I thought I could forget you."

"Why did you marry her, Mikhail? I begged you not to."

"I'll always regret that day. I hated myself for a long time," I say, resting my forehead on hers. "But I felt like I had no choice. The world was stacked against us."

Leah lays her head on my shoulder. "What about now?"

"*Ya by razorval mir radi tebya, moya lyubov.*" (I would tear the world apart for you, my love.)

She smiles against me, using her finger to trace the ink on my chest. The gesture jogs my memory of something I did for her days after my wedding when I heard she left for Spain. Guiding her hand, I place it above my heart and wait for her to read. The tattoo is written in Russian, but Leah seems to have a good grasp of the language.

Using the pad of her finger, she touches the flower and the words carved inside.

"Pretty girl," she whispers, then lifts her watery eyes to mine. "When did you get this done?"

"Four years ago."

"Four years?"

I nod. "If I couldn't have you, I'd have a part of you exactly where you belonged."

Leah wipes at her eyes and lifts up to kiss me. "I never knew you were so romantic, Mikhail Petrov."

Her fingers on my scalp always have my cock at attention.

"It's the most beautiful thing anyone has ever done for me."

Dragging my lips along her neck, I say, "So now you've given me a new goal."

"What's that?" she asks, head tilted, eyes closed as I work toward her ear.

"Topping myself. Everything I give you, everything I do for you—*every* time will be better than the last."

Her smile is radiant. "You don't have to do that."

"No, but I want to. And I will."

"The only thing I want right now is you…and another orgasm."

We laugh, and I dip us under the scalding water when she shivers. Our lips are fused as we break the surface, my tongue gliding against hers, begging for more. But she pulls away, flashes a cunning little smile, and slips beneath the churning bubbles, taking my cock in her hand.

CHAPTER SEVENTEEN
LEAH

The thrum of churning jets drowns out Mikhail's voice above me. His fingers are threaded through my hair, hand guiding me forward over his shaft. While I don't need direction on how to please him, his savage grip only increases my hunger to swallow him until the edges of my vision darken and heighten the euphoria.

Even when my lungs burn and plead for oxygen, I can't pull away. The need to break him with my name on his lips is worth the fire that claws up my throat.

I dig my nails into his thighs and feel him stiffen with every thrust. I know he's close. I just need to push a little more. Tears gather in my eyes, not just because I'm taking him to the limit but because the years of hurt and longing are gone.

He's mine.

"My love," he says on a ragged breath, lifting me above the surface. "Don't drown on me."

I lean into him, my hand taking the place of my mouth while I catch my breath and whisper over his lips. "If I had to die choking on your cock, I'd die the happiest fucking woman on the planet."

"Oh, shit, baby…come here." His kiss is hungry, painful, and delicious. I lose myself momentarily, giving just as good and hard as he is. But when I try to pull away, he protests, so I surprise him by tightening my fingers and squeezing the pressure points just below his jaw.

Mikhail grins, and his eyelids drop, pretty mouth parted as he's coming undone between my hand on his throat and the other around his cock. While I love when he's in control of my body, bending and breaking me to his will, the sight of this man dominated by my touch drives me absolutely fucking feral. I'd leak down my legs if my body weren't submerged underwater.

"You're going to come for me. I want *every* drop," I rasp, biting and tugging his lip.

He nods and lets his head roll back as I dip and take him into my mouth. Both hands clutch my hair, and he bucks his hips, fucking my face.

I love you.

More.

Reaching down, I slip my fingers over my clit, stroking to the rhythm of Mikhail's thrusts until hot spurts of his cum slide down my throat. His grip tightens as he rides the high, and black dots my vision as I climb and crest along with him.

My body is weak from lack of air, and shudders rolling through me, I begin to sink.

But Mikhail's strong arms pull me above the surface and against his heaving chest, where I lay my head and relearn how to breathe.

"You can die a happy woman with my cock in your mouth one day when we're old and gray, but not today."

I chuckle weakly and press a kiss to his neck. "Deal."

The night is quiet, and we sit in each other's arms, letting the heat of the water keep us warm. Being here with him, like this, is almost like a dream.

"What happens tomorrow?"

Mikhail kisses the top of my head. He knows I'm not talking about the drop. My fears lie in the world beyond this place, waiting to tear us apart.

"Tomorrow, you're mine. Always mine."

He shifts me and kisses along my shoulder. "I want you to trust me. There's no going back. I'll spend the rest of my life showing you that the only way we'll ever be apart again is in death."

Goosebumps explode over my skin as he trails snow down my chest and between my breasts.

"Even then, I'll come find you."

"You promise?" I whisper, closing my eyes as the exquisite sensation of ice rolls around my nipple.

"Always."

He laps at the hard peak, warming my skin with his tongue.

"Feels so good," I say, reaching back, my fingers in his hair. "More."

Another small clump of snow traces my breast, circling and forcing my head to loll on his shoulder.

"You're not the only one willing to die happy." Mikhail slides from beneath me and flips me over, pushing my chest onto the snowy deck. "I can't think of a better way to atone for my sins than getting there through your sweet cunt."

CHAPTER EIGHTEEN
LEAH

By the time I woke up this morning, Mikhail was gone. He left a text saying he'd be back by 10 a.m. and to meet him at the cafe for breakfast. Our flight is scheduled for noon, and while we still have a good two hours, I can't help feeling anxious. There's a heaviness in my chest I can't shake, but it's probably because he hasn't answered any of my calls or texts.

Baby, where are you?

I try his cell again, and it goes straight to voicemail this time. Panic begins setting in.

I spring to my feet, not sure where the hell I'm going, but I need to move. I need to feel like I'm doing something—anything to burn this adrenaline.

Mikhail knows no one here. I can't think of a single thing he'd be doing that would keep him away from his phone, much less have it turned off.

Something's wrong.

When I whip around, I slam into what feels like a brick wall. Hands grip my shoulders to the point of pain.

Fuck. Did one of the men from last night find me?

As I reach for my firearm, I see a familiar face staring down at me. Dark eyebrows pinched with annoyance.

"Carlo?"

Carlo is my dad's right-hand man. He's been his partner-slash-bodyguard for years. But what the fuck is he doing here?

Another rush of blood plummets to my toes when I peer around the massive body holding me prisoner.

Papá.

"What…what are you doing here?" I stutter, staring between them in disbelief.

"I think I should be asking you the same, no?"

My father's glare roots me in place. And I suddenly feel like I'm sixteen again. Powerless and entirely at his mercy.

"Do you have any idea the shit I had to pull to find you?"

Carlo steps aside so my father can advance on me, finally releasing his death grip on my arms. However, I'm not sure which of the two is worse.

"Why are you here?"

"Again, that's my question for you."

My father's eyes fall to my neck, nostrils flaring at the telltale redness marking my skin. He shakes his head and narrows his steely gaze, looking at me like I'm the biggest disappointment of his life.

"You've done nothing but sabotage yourself at every turn." Clenching his teeth, he lowers his voice. "You know how hard it will be to find a decent man for you to marry at your age and when you've already been tainted by God knows how many. And now, that fucking Russian bastard, Petrov. I knew I should have taken care of that problem years ago the moment he set his eyes on you." My father grabs my arm, in the same sore spot as Carlo, and I hiss in pain. "But I listened to your brother like a fool. I won't make that mistake twice."

130   ELLE MALDONADO

As he starts dragging me, realization dawns, jolting me awake like a bucket of ice-cold water. With my pulse racing in anguish, I rip my hand from his grasp and stumble back.

"What did you do to him?" I hate how my voice shakes, but it's not out of fear. It's anger and the cloying waves of grief sitting heavy on my chest at the possibility of Mikhail being hurt…or worse.

"Get your ass in the car. And if you dare make a scene—"

"No! I'm not a fucking child anymore. You *won't* dictate my life."

My father's eyes widen with shock and indignation. "Now, tell me. *Where* is he? What did you do?"

I don't care that people are staring and whispering. Not while I'm dying inside and withering in the unknown.

"*Papá*, please." For Mikhail, I'm not beyond begging. "I love him. And if you loved me, you would understand. You know I've felt this way for a long time." Tears stream down my cheeks, but he remains silent, the crease in his features firmly in place. He doesn't give a damn about me or my happiness. To him, it's all about money, power, turf—I'm barely even human in his eyes.

I'm just a walking transaction.

"I hate you," I say from between my teeth.

My father's mouth thins, his jaw tensing. "What the fuck did you just say to me?"

"You heard me. I hate you. And don't act surprised or like you care, because we both know the truth."

"Leah, come with me right now."

I shake my head and shuffle back. "No. I don't want anything to do with you. And when Nikolai finds out what you did…" My voice breaks, and I suck in a tremulous breath. "You deserve everything you have coming."

"You ungrateful little whore. If you think you can disrespect me without consequences—" He signals Carlo with a nod. And although

I try to evade his grasp, he's on me before I can even blink. "You're about to find out what I'm truly capable of. You *will* submit."

Large hands reach into my jacket, then sandwich my arms to my sides, leaving me unable to fight him off.

"I won't! Let me go! I'll kill you."

My pleas for help and my thrashing don't cause a single person to intervene.

Fucking cowards.

He drags me outside, my father leading the way to a black SUV.

"You can't do this. Please. *Papi*, please! Don't do this." I kick at Carlo's thick legs, but the man is solid and doesn't flinch. "Stop! Let me go. *Papá, te lo ruego. Porfavor.*" (Father, please. I'm begging you.)

He doesn't so much as turn around, but simply waves me off with his hand as if I'm unimportant.

"I should have broken you a long time ago." My father's words don't register because, in the next instant, a popping noise explodes near my ear, and I fall onto the cold pavement. While Carlo's hold on me loosens, it isn't enough to disentangle myself from his grip before he takes me down with him. I hit my head on the ground hard enough to feel slightly disoriented.

"Shit," I breathe out, holding my temple. My haze is short-lived when I find myself face-to-face with Carlo's lifeless eyes. The side of his head is drenched in blood, with a bullet wound in the center of the mess.

Gasping, I attempt to crawl away, but another set of solid arms lifts me to my feet. Mikhail shoves me behind him while keeping a gun trained on my father.

"Leah," he growls, muscles so tense he's nearly shaking. I know what he's asking. He's seeking approval to take my father's life.

I squeeze my eyes closed and rest my forehead on his back. As much as I despise everything my father is and his intentions with me…I can't bring myself to do it.

"Let's go. He's not worth the guilt."

Mikhail slides his gaze my way and clamps down on his jaw, neck bobbing as he swallows hard. It takes another five full seconds for him to drop his aim.

"If you ever touch her, look for her—so much as think about her, I'll have your head." Lifting the weapon a second time, Mikhail orders him to strip down to his underwear. My father keeps his stormy gaze pinned on Mikhail as he peels off his suit.

"Looks like I need to phone in a call to Nikolai," he taunts. His grin stretches. "Or rather, Yuri Kosovich."

"Don't tempt me because you already used your one lifeline."

I loop my arm through his. "Please."

It's all he needs to hear. His body visibly relaxes, and he touches my cheek. "Are you okay?"

"I will be."

CHAPTER NINETEEN
MIKHAIL

The moment the car door closes, Leah throws her arms around me and sobs. I pull her into my lap, sure of my decision to have gotten our bags in the car before meeting her at the cafe. While I hate what she went through, it's better Emilio and his man didn't get the jump on me.

"You're okay. I've got you."

Her fist suddenly slams into my chest, then connects a second time. I catch her wrist on the third swing. "What's the matter, my love?"

"I thought you were dead. I thought my father— Mikhail, you weren't there this morning and didn't answer my calls or texts. Where the hell were you?"

I won't lie to her. "Handling the men from the bar."

Her eyes grow wide, and she shakes her head. "Why would you do that on your own? What if—"

"I wasn't. Called in some backup. They helped me take care of things, and they're cleaning up the mess as we speak."

Leah's arms wrap around me again. "You didn't have to do that.

We were leaving."

I pull back and frame her face, our eyes locked so she knows just how serious I am. "I need you to understand I'm not a good man. And there will *never* be a day when someone wrongs you, and I won't rip out their heart while it's still beating."

"Always so romantic," she says with a small laugh, laying her head on my shoulder and going quiet.

I allow her a moment to reflect on what happened with her father. It had taken every ounce of restraint not to mag dump on that son of a bitch. I heard his last words to her.

He doesn't deserve her. But that's fine because Leah is mine now.

The ride to the private airport hangar is quiet. I thought she had fallen asleep for a moment, but I caught her reflection in the window, eyes open, staring hollowly at the passing city.

"We're taking a slight detour," I say, fastening my seatbelt as she does the same beside me. "Stopping at Roman's place in Vegas." Leah watches with rapt attention, waiting for an explanation. "As you know, delayed shipments mean money lost. They want extra for the three-day delay."

"Three days?"

I nod. "They claim we caused a scheduling conflict and needed another day to accommodate their connects. So they say."

"And you're picking up more inventory from Roman?"

"Exactly. Drop is tomorrow at 3 p.m."

Leah pats her pockets, and a look of panic crosses her pretty face. "Fuck."

"What is it?"

"I must have dropped my phone, or maybe Carlo took it. I have to call Ann and Rodri. They have to know what he did—what he tried to do to me."

Rodrigo and I have been close friends for fourteen years. I even consider him a brother. But circumstances have shifted. He's loyal to his father and the business he'll inherit one day, just as I am to mine. Expecting him to throw away everything he's worked to achieve just to side with his sister seems improbable, no matter how deep our ties.

"I hate to suggest this," I say, placing my phone in her hand, ultimately leaving the decision up to her. "But can you trust your brother? I care for him. You know that. But Rod was the only other person who knew our location."

Her features sour, gaze focusing beyond me as she drinks in my words. "He would never…" she whispers, almost to herself. "Would he?"

Leah's eyes find mine, the phone dropping to her lap. Caressing her cheek, I swipe a single tear streaking down her skin.

"A man's heart can be traitorous, given the right incentive, *moya lyubov'*. And Rodrigo is ambitious, with a desire for power and wealth that rivals your father's."

"If he sold me out, I'll never forgive him."

"We'll figure it out. I promise."

She kisses me. "Thank you for what you did back there."

"Don't thank me, because the things I'm capable of doing for you would scare you. They scare me sometimes."

She smiles, pressing another sweet kiss to my lips. "I love you. And you don't scare me, Mikhail. You complete me."

LAS VEGAS, NEVADA

Roman answers the door, his new wife beside him, and greets me in the only way a younger brother would. "You look like shit."

I chuckle and pull him in for a hug, clapping his back a little harder than he probably expects.

"Yeah, well, it's been a shit morning," I say, threading my fingers through Leah's as we cross the threshold.

His wife, Nadia, greets us warmly, and we exchange introductions. While Leah and Roman have met in passing, their interactions were nothing beyond a cordial hello and goodbye. He's heard what he knows of her through me, but mostly the broken version of us, post-Leah.

The women opt to remain upstairs while Roman and I take a winding staircase to a hidden cellar below the main floor landing.

"I'm glad to see your ball sack finally dropped," he jokes as he punches a code into the slate metal door. "I was worried you were trying to be like Dad and swearing off women for a decade after that whole Celeste bullshit. Lev and I were *this* close to staging a goddamn intervention to get you some pussy, brother."

I can't help but laugh. "Don't be a dick. Getting pussy wasn't exactly the problem. But I'm flattered you care."

Roman slides a black crate from beneath a shelf and flips open the lid. "This enough?"

I peer inside and take a quick mental inventory, nodding my approval.

"I wired the funds to your account and threw in a little extra as a thank-you and, of course, a wedding gift."

"You didn't have to do that, but I appreciate it."

I observe my brother for a beat. Something is different about him. He's still the same cheeky bastard as always, but he seems more... grounded and happier. The most telling is in the way he looks at his wife like she's the only one in the room.

A feeling I know all too well.

"It looks good on you—married life, settling down. Never thought I'd see the day."

Roman chuckles. "You know how it is. What's that saying? Life throws you curve balls and all that shit. Well, I got clocked in the goddamn face, and I liked it."

We share another laugh.

"And you," he says. "It's good to see you finally found your way back to her."

"I did."

Roman reaches for a decanter. "Yeah, I was tired of listening to you cry like a little bitch."

I slap the back of his head like I used to when we were kids. Our laughter reminds me that I need to visit more often. Now that I have to move out of Texas, that might just be the case.

The mood suddenly shifts, as if we're reading each other's thoughts. I already briefed him on everything that happened with Emilio during our flight.

"You should have wasted him, Mikhail. One less reason to look over your shoulder," he says, pouring a glass of whiskey and sliding it across the table.

I shake my head and sigh. "At the end of the day, that's still her father. I didn't want that kind of shit hanging over our heads."

"You tell Dad yet?"

"Not yet. But we should spread the word and be on alert, just in case. Something tells me I'll be seeing him sooner than expected."

Roman tips his glass. "Agreed."

CHAPTER TWENTY
LEAH

Mikhail's phone has been buzzing for what seems like the one-hundredth time in the last two hours. Between Ann and Rodri calling nonstop, I'm slowly losing it. Mikhail's words about my brother still resonate, and as much as it pains me, I know his advice is sound. While Ann has always had a fractured relationship with our father, she's close to Mom, who is as loyal to her husband as they come, no matter what.

It's not something I'm prepared to deal with, especially after I've had time to let it all sink in.

Mikhail raps twice on the bathroom door before pushing it open. "Pizza is here."

I grab my sleep shorts from the vanity, but he snatches them.

"What are you doing?" I ask with a suspicious grin.

"You don't need them." He cocks his head, eyes falling to my black panties. "I like those better." Leaning against the door frame and crossing his arms over his bare chest, he says, "Turn around."

"Really?" I pretend to be offended, hands on my hips.

"The faster you show me my ass, the sooner you get to eat, pretty girl. I'm just trying to see what's on the menu for dessert."

A smile curves my lips as I lift my shirt and do as I'm told. I'm not wearing a thong, but they're plenty cheeky, nonetheless.

"Nah," Mikhail says, shaking his head in disapproval.

"Mikhail!" I shriek, slightly offended. "Listen, this is a great ass, okay? Someone clearly does not want dessert."

He barks a laugh and lunges for me, hauling me on his waist, a hand on each cheek. "Perfect…if it wasn't missing my handprints."

"I'm surprised they've faded. You have some big fucking hands, Mikki," I tease, leaning in for a kiss when his phone vibrates in his pocket.

He pulls out the device and blocks every number associated with my family.

"Are you okay?" he asks as he kisses my forehead.

I sigh and gently scratch the back of his nape, reveling in how his features relax with my touch. "Yeah, I am. The world and all its shit can wait. We need to have our game faces on and get through tomorrow first. For now, the only thing I want is pizza and your cock. Simple."

"Good, because I'm craving the same."

"Pizza and cock?"

Leaving his phone behind, he laughs and bites my earlobe as we make our way to the kitchen. "I'm definitely reddening that ass tonight."

"Don't make me beg," I murmur against his mouth.

"That's the best part."

"Oh?" I say, peppering kisses up his jaw.

"*Moya krasivitsa*, you begging on your knees to suck my cock and on all fours begging to get fucked…" He sucks in a sharp breath. "I promise you, I have never seen anything more beautiful."

I kiss him hard, and my worries melt away with every stroke of his tongue, nip of his teeth, and the way he tastes so damn good. He's my safe space, where nothing can touch me as long as I'm in his arms.

"What kind of pizza did you order?"

Mikhail deposits me on the counter next to the pizza box and throws it open. "Your favorite: Hawaiian."

"Baby, you hate pineapple on your pizza." I giggle, recalling the day I made him taste it for the first time.

"*Eto chertova tragediya.*" (It's a goddamn tragedy.)

I tip my head back and burst into another bout of laughter. "Well, now I feel bad."

"You should!" he jokes, bringing a slice to my mouth. I take an exaggerated bite and melted cheese stretches, breaking off against my chin. Luckily for me, the pizza isn't piping hot.

Twinkling suddenly catch my eye from the balcony of Mikhail's condo, where multi-colored Christmas lights are wrapped along the railing.

"Your balcony is festive. Did you put those up?"

"No, I have someone who cleans this place for me: Caroline. She always decorates according to the season when she knows I'll be in town. Says it's for morale, whatever that hell means."

"I'm pretty sure it has nothing to do with the brooding, if-looks-could-kill expression that lives on your handsome face."

He chucks a piece of pineapple at me, and I pluck it off my t-shirt with a laugh and pop it into my mouth.

"*Ty khochesh' byt' nakazannym segodnya vecherom, ne tak li?*" (You want to get punished tonight, don't you?)

Without waiting for a response, Mikhail snatches me off the counter, pizza in hand, and tosses me onto the sofa.

"You said pizza and cock, pretty girl, but never specified in what order."

Shoving my shirt up over my breasts, my words disintegrate

when he bites down on a nipple and rolls the other between his fingers. I indulge in his touch, lip between my teeth with every flick of his tongue and how his hard body presses against my pussy. But I told him I wanted his cock, and I wasn't lying.

I roll us over, and we tumble off the couch in a heap of laughter. Throwing my leg over him, I straddle his torso and lean down to lick where my nickname is inked on his chest.

"Maybe you didn't hear me the first time," I say, kissing down the toned lines of his stomach, past his navel, and biting the waistband of his sweatpants where his dick rages to break out.

Mikhail grins and folds his arms behind his head. "Please, jog my memory."

As I pull at his pants, his cock springs free. There's a moment of hesitation as I drink in the sight of him and think to myself that the science behind how this particular organ fits inside my body is something to be studied.

Biting my lip in anticipation, I dip to his thigh and brush against his skin. He tenses, waiting for me to make contact, but I choose to have a little fun first.

A trail of soft kisses toward his groin sees him closing his eyes and cursing under his breath. But just as I'm about to graze his pulsing erection, I switch and press my lips to the opposite inner thigh.

"Leah, my cock ain't gonna suck itself."

"Leah? I thought we were past that, Mikki. You better ask nicer than that," I tease with a grin, swiping the precum off his tip and dipping my tongue, fiending for more.

In a flash, Mikhail fists my hair, the sting ripping a gasp from my chest as he pulls me closer while also grasping his dick and using it to slap me hard against the cheek.

"Mikhail!" I half-chuckle and whine. But my protest earns me another cock slap.

Fuck.

The impact vibrates through me, down to my throbbing pussy, making my entire body hum.

Without a moment to recover, he slams me over his dick and pushes to the back of my throat. I gag at the massive intrusion, and it only spurs him on.

"It's like you're singing a song for me, *moya lyubov'*," he says, guiding my movements and pumping his hips. Through the haze of tears, I see my ruined slice of dinner overturned on the carpet beside us.

Tragic pizza can wait.

CHAPTER TWENTY ONE
LEAH

Fuck. Fuck. Fuck.

My body is on fire. Every inch burning hotter, buzzing as a scream crawls up my throat, unable to escape the confines of a dream. But I don't want to wake up.

Possibly ever.

It feels too good, too fucking good.

Please, let me die here, I beg, to no one—to everyone.

I rock my hips and let my thighs fall open as an expert devourer of cunts ravages my pussy. Every cell in my body is electric, the sensation reaching deep, igniting my soul.

"Don't…stop," I breathe, finally breaking through the veil of sleep.

"Good morning, pretty girl." His mouth moves against my clit, forcing another gasp from my lips.

"M-Mikhail…" My voice is slightly hoarse as I lift my head and blink away the last shred of confusion.

And there he is—this beautiful man—*my* beautiful man, waking me up in the best way imaginable. "God, I love you," I moan, my head falling against the pillow as he angles my hips and licks me from end to fucking end.

I make a motion to reach for his luscious head of hair, and that's when I realize my arms are tied above my head—with fucking Christmas lights. In a simultaneous dawn of awareness, I attempt to bring my legs together, but they're also restrained by the multi-colored lights that once decorated the balcony railing.

"You didn't think I wouldn't follow through on my word, did you?" Mikhail rises, mouth and beard glistening with my arousal. "I've had a lot of fun playing with this pretty pussy. And so did you. Came for me once already."

"You're a bastard," I chuckle between moans. "And I love it."

"*Krasivaya devushka*, your body knows who it belongs to, even in sleep." Without breaking eye contact, he uses the flat of his tongue to lick up my slit. My mouth parts, legs shuddering. "You sang for me, came for me." Mikhail drops kisses on my aching center, eyes still watching the way he makes my face contort with sinful pleasure. "So beautiful, Leah. So goddamn gorgeous. Like a horny little Christmas tree."

We laugh at that. But my humor fades as the fire inside grows hotter while his movements slow.

"Fuck…baby…what is…I can't…" My words fail as I arch off the bed, and an orgasm rockets through me. Taking advantage of my vulnerable position, Mikhail brings his tongue back to my pussy and slides two fingers inside as I squirm and cry out, at the mercy of his sweet torture.

But he doesn't relent, even as I'm nearly crawling out of my skin and climbing the high of another release.

"No, no…no, baby, no…" I moan and try to clamp my legs closed. And that's when I feel the fullness I haven't registered until now.

Son of a bitch found my butt plug.

"You went through…my black bag," I murmur, head lolling.

He laughs darkly. "You came prepared, didn't you?" Mikhail squeezes my nipple and circles my clit with his tongue.

I thrash against my restraints, needing to run, scream, die, and come all at once.

"You knew you were coming to collect what was yours," he says between strokes. "What's always been yours."

"Fuck…Mikki. Too much!"

"Again. You can take it. I want to feel you squeeze me with this pretty cunt until you've made a mess on the sheets, and you're dripping from my mouth."

Three fingers inside me now, he hooks and licks with more vigor, bringing me to the fringes of an explosion and filling me so wholly, yet I would give anything to swallow his cock at the same time. My mouth waters at the thought despite the bruises still fresh in my throat from last night.

"More, my love," he urges, increasing the vibrations on the butt plug.

"Shit," I cry as my hips buck to meet his thrusts.

Faster.

Another notch and the jolt catapults me into a toe-curling orgasm. When my release splashes on my thighs and belly, I know I gave him exactly what he wanted.

But Mikhail isn't done. He's ravenous, fingers buried, leaving their mark as he drinks me down and savors every drop.

"Yes…yes, baby…" I whine, my hips still moving, still fucking his face and riding out the last waves of pleasure.

He tilts my ass and runs his tongue up each cheek.

"My girl's greedy little cunt is still begging for more."

I lazily shake my head as he kisses up my body and rises to his knees, reaching for a blade on the nightstand and cutting the cords connecting my legs to the bedpost. I wait for him to free my hands, but instead, he dips down, lips on mine, and devours my mouth.

The taste of my cum, coupled with the vibration still sparking through my body, ignites another fire. I curl my leg around his waist, desperate for friction, even if it kills me.

"There she is," he rasps. Biting my shoulder, he reaches between us, grabbing his rock-hard cock and stroking the head against my swollen clit.

"Fuck me, Mikhail," I beg, lifting my hips.

But he pulls away, making me want to quite literally kill him. So I yank at the damn cords around my wrists and groan, "Untie me. Now."

"Not yet," he replies with a devious smirk, then drops a fleeting kiss on my lips before flipping me over on my hands and knees. "Grab on to the headboard."

I don't hesitate and assume the position, back arched and ass up, desperate to be full of him. But again, he toes the line between life and death when he climbs off the bed and heads toward the window.

The sun has barely peaked the horizon, so the light filtering inside the room is minimal, but he closes the blackout curtains regardless, bathing us in shadows—except for the lights twinkling around my wrists.

And when I glance back, the blue light in my asshole glitters.

"*Krasivyy.*" (Beautiful.)

"You owe me for this," I say, trying to suppress a smile.

Mikhail laughs, crawling in behind me, gripping my cheeks, and spreading them open. "Fuck, Leah," he growls as he tightens his hold.

"Yeah, yeah, your horny Christmas tree here needs to get fucked before you die, Mr. Petrov."

He barks a laugh as his lips journey up my spine. "I'm taking this tight little hole, too," he says, nudging the head of his cock against the butt plug.

"It's yours, baby. Whenever you want it." A moan rolls off my tongue as he pushes inside, spreading me open, the sensation deliciously painful. "I'm yours."

"Always mine. *Moya krasavitsa*."

CHAPTER TWENTY TWO
MIKHAIL

Wet gravel crunches beneath the tires as we roll into a warehouse parking lot. The building is one of three locations frequently used by my men for shipments. It operates on a port under the guise of a spring factory.

The routine is ingrained in us: arrive early, park with an easy escape route, watch our six, wait, and wait some more. But today's drop feels…off. A different type of energy permeates the air, heightening our anticipation.

I slide a gaze to Leah, who's staring at my phone screen and flipping it every few breaths. She doesn't seem nervous, but it's obvious her mind is elsewhere. In this business, we need to check all of life's issues at the door and be on alert and prepared for the unexpected. While this faction is known to me and my family, with countless transactions in the past, I'll never let my guard down. And today rings true more than ever when my whole heart is sitting beside me, counting on me for a seamless drop so that we're able to move on and face whatever lies ahead.

"Shouldn't be too much longer now," I reassure her, taking her hand in mine.

She nods, eyes back on my phone.

"Should be a quick exchange if you want to stay in the car—"

Leah snaps her head in my direction. "Don't do that, Mikhail. Not you."

Reaching across the middle console, I stroke her cheek. "*Moya lyubov'*, it's not what you're thinking. I know you have a lot on your mind."

"And I bet you have just the same on yours. I'm here for a reason, and I've done this before, Mikhail."

"I have enemies."

She narrows her brown eyes. "Liar."

"That's not a lie."

"No, you lied about your reason for asking me to hang back. Bringing up your enemies solidifies that."

"I love you, and I'm always going to worry about you, whether you're here or at a goddamn grocery store. My family has enemies, just as sure as yours. You're everything, pretty girl. You have no idea how many sacks of shit would love to exploit Emilio's little gem."

She opens her mouth in protest, but I shush her with a kiss. "Turned Mikhail Petrov's wife."

A broad smile lights up her beautiful face.

"Did you marry me while I was sleeping too?"

I laugh and tug her toward me by her nape. "Don't give me ideas. We can always fly back to Vegas and be married by dinner."

"As tempting as that sounds, wouldn't it be crazy for you to head to your father's reunion a married man? He'll be wondering where the hell your new wife is."

"What do you mean? You'll be by my side, second to my father and his wife at the head of the table. Like a queen, exactly where you belong."

It's her turn to look confused. "Mikhail, I can't just..." Her expression sours. "What if they don't..."

I tip her chin, forcing our eyes to meet. "If they don't, what, like you? Accept you?" She nods. "Leah, they'll accept you on principle because you're *mine*, and I love you."

"Mikhail, I'm not like Celeste."

"No, the fuck you're not, because she was the biggest mistake of my life. I hurt you, and I lost you when I should have fought for you. You're the woman I want to wake up to until the day I die." I push a loose strand of hair behind her ear and kiss her forehead. "And I can't wait to make babies with you."

Leah's eyes glisten with unshed tears. "You know, you're pretty sappy for a mafia boss," she jokes, fisting my collar and pulling me to her lips.

"I'm going to dress you up like a fuck doll for Halloween, then stuff every hole like a goddamn turkey and make you my horny little Christmas tree every year."

She laughs and squeezes my face, peppering kisses along my jaw. "That's better."

The blissful moment comes crashing down when my phone chimes, signaling their arrival.

"You know the drill if things go south."

A flash of defiance crosses her features, and she hesitates but eventually nods. It's for show since we know neither one of us is capable of leaving the other behind, even if given the chance.

My men unload the inventory onto trolleys and take the lead as we head toward a side entrance. Leah and I keep a sizable distance between us as a precautionary measure to avoid exploiting weaknesses. With a quick wink, she crosses the threshold of the building, and I offer a reassuring nod before stealing a sweeping glance behind me as I follow her inside.

The long corridor is equipped with surveillance at every angle, the feed funneling through to my home and a cloud server accessible by my father. Apart from the low thrum of a ventilation system and the clicks of Leah's boots, the building is quiet. Nothing different from previous transactions, but the sense of heightened awareness and slight paranoia has me on higher alert than usual.

My men glance back, seeking my approval, before pushing open the double doors at the end of the hall. Giving them the okay, I hustle forward, my arm on Leah's as I take her place. She falls back without protest.

"In and out, my love," I whisper. "Tomorrow, we'll be in Chicago. Together."

The hint of a smile moves across her face until she peers past me, and it's replaced by hard lines and all business. Taking her cue, I follow suit.

Isaac Bianchi, underboss for the local Italian faction, has been in business with my family for a number of years. It's rare for him to attend a simple exchange such as this one, let alone flanked by five men too many. Blood rushes past my ears as I mentally begin to calculate a plan of attack. The building is outfitted with safe rooms, trapdoors, and tunnels for instances of betrayal or a raid.

"Mikhail Petrov," he says, lighting a cigar. "Glad to see you finally made it." His eyes flicker to Leah and narrow. "Rodrigo sent in one hell of a replacement."

"Inventory is all there, plus the extra you requested."

Rage crawls up the back of my neck with each second his gaze stays on my girl. I need to divert his attention away from Leah and get the hell out of here before I do something stupid that ends up getting us both killed.

"Patience, Mikhail. There's no rush. Unless you have somewhere more important to be."

"I do," I deadpan.

Isaac belts out a laugh. "I'm sure you do. Though I don't blame you; I'd be in a hurry to get the fuck out of here, too, if I had that sweet piece of ass waiting for me."

I suck in a sharp breath, my muscles tensing. "Don't," I grit out between clenched teeth.

He chuckles, idly staring at his cigar, then points it at me as he speaks. "The big, bad Mikhail Petrov thinks he has some kind of power here. But unfortunately for you, you don't have the upper hand, friend. So I suggest you relax, and we can all go home when this is over."

The Beretta at my side is heavy and hot, and the urge to put a hole through his face is making my hands shake with anticipation.

"Now, I just need to know who I'm doing business with. That's all," he says as he moves toward Leah.

I ball my fist, jaw so tight I'm one ounce of pressure away from cracking teeth.

"I haven't heard you say a single word, sweetheart. A little too pretty for this line of work. But given that you're here, I'm assuming there's a reason."

Leah doesn't break. She maintains eye contact and slow blinks at his remarks.

"What's your name, *bella?*"

He reaches a hand up, as if intending to caress her face, but she dodges his touch and levels him with a cold glare.

"Cut the bullshit. Your product is all there. Confirm so we can end this."

A grin so wide I see his capped molars splits his face. He twists around. "I like her. Must be a little firecracker in the sheets—"

"Enough!" I growl, leaning in his direction. A chorus of chambering bullets follows.

"Relax, Mikhail," he warns. "All I wanted to say is that you are one lucky son of a bitch to bag yourself the daughter of Emilio Castellanos."

Hearing her father's name finally breaks her mask of indifference. Her eyebrows knit together in confusion.

"You know I'm a businessman, Petrov. I don't keep emotional ties with anyone outside my circle. I owe you and your father nothing. So when Yuri Kosovich rings and makes me an offer, who am I to refuse?"

"Son of a bitch."

"I won't deny that," he says with a chuckle. "But wait, it gets better. Imagine my surprise when Emilio himself doubles that offer in exchange for your head and the return of his precious little *Leah*."

In the next second, Leah's gun is pressed against Isaac's forehead.

A gesture that only widens his smile. "If you think that's wise, I encourage you to pull the trigger."

"Fuck you. I'd rather die."

"Well, I'm glad we're on the same page, *bella*, because the moment you walked in, I knew, without a doubt, I was going to keep you for myself."

"The hell you are," I roar, reaching for my gun as the barrels of five others train on me.

"On your knees, Petrov. Do as you're told, and this will be quick and painless. Otherwise, I can be creative."

Leah lowers her weapon and shifts her wary gaze to me, shaking her head. "I'll go with you. Wherever you want, just don't hurt him."

"No, fuck that! You touch her, I'll take your goddamn head."

"Mikhail, no," she counters. "Please, for me."

Isaac disarms her and chuckles. "How touching. But I'm not here to negotiate, and you may be pretty as sin, but you don't set the terms here."

He motions to two of his men, and they approach Leah. I lunge for her but drop to the ground when Isaac presses his Glock to her temple.

"I have more wet cunt waiting for me at home than you can imagine. I'm not too invested here. Pussy is pussy, so don't test me." He digs the barrel harder against her skull. "Knees, now."

Despair grips my heart, and I fall to my knees.

"Take her to the car."

Leah locks eyes with me, and where I expect to see tears, there's fire.

"I love you," she says, twisting the gun out of Isaac's hand and rapid-firing two bullets into the two men at her side. They hit the ground, and the warehouse descends into chaos.

My men, previously standing like useless bastards, begin firing their weapons as I crawl behind a metal beam, sending gunfire into the crowd.

"Leah!" Calling out to her is sure to give away my position, but I don't give a damn. Nothing matters to me but her safety.

What feels like a metal pipe connects to the side of my head, and pain ripples across my face. One of Isaac's men is on me in the next beat and clocks me with a solid right hook before I can get my bearings. Blood spills inside my mouth as another hit splits my lip. As he comes in for the finishing blow, I wrap my hands around his throat and squeeze, but he pulls a knife, aiming for my face.

The sound of a single gunshot blares in my ear when it pierces the side of his head, and he slumps over.

"Leah, baby." I tug her behind the beam and frame her face as bullets ricochet around us. "Are you okay?"

"Yeah. You?" she asks, swiping her thumb against my bloody lip.

"Of course. You need to get out of here. I'll cover you."

"Let's not waste our last moments arguing over something pointless. I'm not leaving you. We fight, we die, but we do it together."

I would drag her out myself if I could, but I know she won't budge.

"God, I love you," I say, kissing her forehead. "I'm sorry I wasted so much time. We would have been like five kids deep by now."

Leah and I share a teary, half-hearted laugh.

"When this is all over. When we…" Her voice breaks. "Come find me, baby."

I slam my mouth onto hers and kiss her as if it's the last time. Because it is.

"*Ya tebya lyublyu.*"

"Te amo."

With one last kiss, we jump to our feet, prepared to go out fighting. But as we aim our weapons, a barrage of automatic gunfire explodes, and we hit the floor. A deafening silence follows until hurried footfalls echo in our direction.

"Leah? Mikhail?"

Leah's eyes widen as Rodrigo's voice rings out. Her hard pants raise the dust around our faces as she looks at me, unsure of what to do. If he's here to take her from me, he'll have to pry her from my dead hands.

"Leah," he calls, his tone softer now. "Please don't be dead. Papá is lucky I haven't slit his fucking throat and hung him from a bridge. But if he made me…"

There's a crack in his voice, and Leah doesn't hesitate.

"Rodri?"

His gun falls beside him as she runs into his arms. "How about you answer your goddamn phone?" he says, lifting her off the floor in a tight hug.

Letting them have their moment, I breathe a sigh of relief until I spot movement in my peripheral. And a grin crooks the side of my mouth.

Isaac attempts to drag himself across the floor, sliding in a pool of his own blood. I kneel beside him and toss him onto his back.

"If you keep moving at this pace, I'm sure you'll make it to the door before bleeding out."

He tries to speak, but gags on the blood dripping out of his mouth.

"You had a lot to say earlier when you were disrespecting my girl, and I can't let that slide, Isaac. You owe me your tongue." I pat my pockets. "Lucky for you, I didn't bring my blade." I grip my fingers around his throat. "But don't worry, I can be creative."

I squeeze into his neck until the skin ruptures, and his mouth gapes in a silent scream. He claws at my arm, but I keep digging and tearing flesh as he shudders and uselessly tries to fight me off.

"Ah, there it is." The squelching sound of muscle tearing fills me with a sense of satisfaction. *"Uvidimsya v adu."* (See you in hell.)

Isaac is still twitching as I straighten and toss his goddamn tongue across the room where everything went to shit.

None of that matters when I find the smiling face of the woman I love. The world can crumble and burn to ash around us, but as long as she's by my side, there's always a tomorrow.

EPILOGUE
MIKHAIL

Chicago, Illinois

Waves of dark hair fall down her back as she twists in front of the mirror, hands smoothing down a fitted white dress—the third one she's tried on in the last hour. Uncertainty flashes across her face, and she reaches toward the zipper at her side with a sigh of defeat.

"Don't you dare take that off."

Leah startles and whips around. "I'm not sure it's the right one—" she says as she returns to her reflection.

I stalk toward her, sweeping the hair from her shoulders and dropping kisses along her skin.

"What's the matter, my love? You look— *Fuck*, you look exquisite."

She closes her eyes and leans into my chest. "I'm nervous, Mikhail. Your father knows who I am and everything I represent to you, your family, and his empire. I'm afraid he won't accept me. Neither will your brothers. Especially when they find out my father has allied with Yuri."

"Look at me." After a beat of hesitation, she meets my eyes in the mirror. "My family will welcome you with open arms because you're the woman I love. They all know what happened and are still excited to meet you. I promise. And Roman and Nadia will be there."

She sighs and nods, eyes back on the dress. "I trust you."

"And even if by some twist of fate, they don't. It changes nothing, pretty girl." I dip to her ear. "Remember what I said, I'll burn it all down for you."

Leah lets herself melt into my arms. "I love you."

"And you should know, the only reason I haven't peeled you out of this goddamn dress is because I promised my father I'd attend." I tug her closer, my cock hard on her back. "Otherwise, you'd be naked right now, on that table, spread open for me, while I enjoy my own little Christmas dinner."

Leah turns around, a riveting smile curving her plush mouth. "We better hurry back home, then."

"I think it's cute that you think I won't have you before the night's end."

Laughing, she rises to her toes and kisses me. "If you think we're having sex at your father's house, you're dead wrong."

"Challenge accepted."

"Mikhail, no! Absolutely not." I lift her and throw her over my shoulder before she can stop me. "What are you doing?" she asks, breaking into fits of laughter.

"The sooner we leave, the sooner I eat."

RESIDENCE OF NIKOLAI & NATALIA PETROV

I see my father kiss his wife, tenderly touching her rounded belly before she says her goodbyes and leaves the office. Despite my initial reservations due to their age gap, he's never looked happier. Glancing at my girl beside me, I realize I'm no one to judge. And I can't help feeling overjoyed that he's found someone to lift him from the darkness after a decade and give him things he thought he'd never have.

Baby Norah will be here soon, and she'll be the most spoiled and protected baby in Chicago.

"*Mikhail*," he says in Russian, "you're welcome to stay until we secure assets and reinforce our allies and businesses in Texas."

My arm instinctively curls around Leah's waist.

"And, of course, you too, Leah," he says, the corners of his eyes creasing with a smile.

When he officially accepts the woman I love, the weight of some unknown stress, one I didn't know I carried, lifts from my shoulders.

"Thank you," she replies, returning his smile.

My father rounds his massive desk and claps my chest. "Dinner is in about thirty minutes. The keys and paperwork to your property are in my top drawer if you want to take a look."

"We'll catch up," I say as he exits.

"That went better than I thought it would."

"I knew he'd love you."

I pull open the desk drawer and search for the paperwork he mentioned.

"Don't get ahead of yourself, Mikki. It's only day one."

When I pull the file with my name, a white and blue box hidden beneath it draws my attention. I couldn't be happier for my dad and his wife, but I sure as fuck don't want the visuals coming to mind when I stumble on his stash of lube.

"That old, dirty bastard."

Leah's mouth hangs open, amusement lighting up her face. "Are you talking about your dad?

"Yeah," I laugh, tossing her the unopened package.

Caught off guard, she scrambles to catch it mid-air, then bursts into laughter. "Mikhail! Why are you touching your dad's lube? Let that man live."

I set the files down and reach for her, tucking her body between my legs as I lean on the edge of the desk. "I don't blame him. I'm still going to be bending, breaking, and ravaging you every fucking chance I get when I'm his age."

"Are you?" she says, levering up to kiss me.

"I'll never get tired of your pretty cunt, my love." If there are only two things I can give her in life, they would be orgasms and reasons to make her laugh.

"Good to know."

I glance at my watch. "We have twenty-five minutes."

"Until dinner?"

"No, for you to let me fold you over this desk and put that little box to good use."

She shakes her head, a smile from ear to ear. "Not happening, Mikki."

As she attempts to pull away, I tug her back and push her body against the wood, my hand sliding up her thigh. "I've been walking around all goddamn night with a hard-on because of this little dress. You've noticed me eye-fucking you, haven't you, pretty girl? And I know you like it."

"No," she whispers, spreading her thighs for me.

I slip a finger into her thong, and she's soaking wet. "Liar."

"*Fuck.*"

"There it is. That's my girl. Open up a little more." Pushing her chest against the desk, I shove the sinful dress above her ass. "So fucking beautiful, *moya lyubov'*."

"Mikhail…the door isn't locked, baby."

"You want me to lock it?" I ask as I kiss up the back of her thigh.

"Yes!"

I chuckle and stroke her clit. "Why? Because you want me to fuck you right here on this desk?"

"Mikhail," she begs, jolting when I slap her needy little cunt.

"Say it." Another crack between her legs has her crying out and clawing at the wooden surface.

"Yes… Fuck me, please."

"*Eto moya khoroshaya devochka.*" (That's my good girl.)

I drop to my knees to worship her and grip the edges of her thong, sliding it down her legs until it's stretched around her ankles. "Leave this here," I say, kissing and nipping my way back up.

"Your dad…will kill us."

"Me? Yes." I run my tongue along her slit. "You? No one touches you."

Leah pounds the desk when I push my fingers inside and play with that spot that causes a mess. But as much as I love to watch every drop flow out of her, not here.

The sealed white and blue box catches my eye, and I snatch and tear it open.

"Mikhail, you fucker…put that back!"

She attempts to straighten, but I shove her down. "He'll never know," I say as I squeeze the tube between her cheeks and stroke her clit to keep her complacent.

"What are you doing, baby?" Her voice is barely above a whisper the higher I take her.

"I want this tight ass. Can I do that, *moya krasavitsa*? Can I take this?"

Leah's eyes are squeezed shut, thighs trembling, and my cock is about to put a hole through the goddamn front of my pants at such a beautiful sight.

Her nod is slow as she agonizes under my touch. I move quickly to free my dick and glide it along her wet entrance before nudging at the muscles of her ass.

"Easy, pretty girl. Relax." Another squirt of the stolen lube, and I push forward as she whines. "Make yourself feel good," I urge, stretching her inch by inch.

Leah does as she's told and touches herself. The more she strokes, the more she relaxes, and the deeper I sink until I'm buried as far as she can take me.

"Fuck, you're doing so good, pretty girl. But you're going to have to be quiet."

"Mikhail, don't stop…or I'll kill you."

I retreat from inside her with a laugh before sinking again and again. It's so fucking tight, so damn good my legs shake, and my balls coil tighter with every stroke.

We're beyond the stage of caring who hears, not that it would matter because I'm sure every single soul in this house knows what's going down in this room. I'll deal with my father's wrath later.

The only thing that matters is the woman beneath me, her tight ass swallowing my cock as she cries out my name, and we fall over the edge into sweet oblivion.

Moments later, we're on the floor, my back against the infamous desk, my girl resting between my legs.

"I can't go out there. I'm going to have to live here now," she deadpans.

My laughter shakes her body.

"I'm glad you find this funny."

"My love, all my brothers are filthy sons of bitches. They don't care."

She whirls around. "I care! How will I face your dad when he just met me as your girlfriend, and I got fucked in his office? And with his lube!"

I caress her cheek. "Do you think it would make a difference if you were my fiancée and I fucked you in his office?"

"Mikki, be serious."

"I'm so fucking serious." I take her hand and slide a solitaire diamond on her finger, fit for a queen.

Leah stares at the ring in stunned silence, tears welling in her eyes.

"Marry me."

She tackles me to the floor, kissing me hard. "Ask me again."

I smile against her lips. "Will you marry me?"

"Again," she whispers, her tears breaking off the tip of her nose and onto my cheek.

I roll us over and use my thumb to wipe her eyes.

"Leah Castellanos, will you do me the honor of being my wife?"

She smiles and pulls me in for another kiss. "It's about damn time."

THE END

Mikhail Petrov is part of The Petrov Family anthology:

Nikolai Petrov by M.A. Cobb

Roman Petrov by Luna Mason
Viktor by Darcy Embers
Lev Petrov by Harper-Lee Rose
Aleksei Petrov by M.L. Hargy

OTHER WORKS
BY ELLE MALDONADO

The Severed Signet Series

Severed by Vengeance – Forbidden Romance
Book 1
https://mybook.to/aPXnbC

Tempted by Blood – Enemies to Lovers
Book 2
https://mybook.to/nTJf

Bound by Betrayal – Marriage of Convenience
Book 3
https://mybook.to/PqAy8i

Liberated by Sin
Book 4
January 2025
https://mybook.to/C2D2v

Tempted by Blood: The Chase
Novella
https://mybook.to/aoQj

*Leni and Silas are back on an extreme scavenger hunt, **collecting contracts** around the globe.*
Winner takes all.
Leni doesn't play by the rules and has no intention of going easy on the man she loves—even if it means drawing a little blood.
But Silas is on a mission, ready for her brand of beautiful mayhem. The stakes are high, and he's got his eye on the ultimate prize.

ABOUT
ELLE MALDONADO

Elle Maldonado writes dark, contemporary romance. She lives in the U.S. with her husband and three kids and enjoys spending time with family, watching movies, and reading.

Subscribe to her newsletter and join my Facebook group for all upcoming releases, sneak peeks, giveaways, teasers, and extra scenes.

https://tr.ee/t5xCxlh6hc

https://linktr.ee/authorellemaldonado

Made in the USA
Columbia, SC
08 April 2025

56240593R00102